KING OF SHADOWS

Also by Susan Cooper

In The Dark Is Rising sequence:

Over Sea, Under Stone
(An Aladdin Paperback)

The Dark Is Rising
The 1974 Newbery Honor Book

Greenwitch

The Grey King
Winner of the 1976 Newbery Medal

Silver on the Tree

(Margaret K. McElderry Books)

The Boggart
An ALA Notable Children's Book

The Boggart and the Monster

Danny and the Kings
illustrated by Jos. A. Smith

Dawn of Fear
(An Aladdin Paperback)

Dreams and Wishes: Essays on Writing for Children

Matthew's Dragon
illustrated by Jos. A. Smith

Seaward
(An Aladdin Paperback)

The Silver Cow: A Welsh Tale
illustrated by Warwick Hutton
(An Aladdin Paperback)

Tam Lin
illustrated by Warwick Hutton

(Margaret K. McElderry Books)

KING OF SHADOWS

SUSAN COOPER

Aladdin Paperbacks

New York   London   Toronto   Sydney   Singapore

If you purchased this book without a cover you should be aware that this book is stolen property. It was reported as "unsold and destroyed" to the publisher and neither the author nor the publisher has received any payment for this "stripped book."

First Aladdin Paperbacks edition June 2001

Copyright © 1999 by Susan Cooper

Aladdin Paperbacks
An imprint of Simon & Schuster
Children's Publishing Division
1230 Avenue of the Americas
New York, NY 10020

All rights reserved, including the right of reproduction in whole or in part in any form.

Also available in a Margaret K. McElderry Books hardcover edition
Designed by Ann Bobco

The text for this book was set in Berkeley.

Printed and bound in the United States of America

10 9 8 7 6

The Library of Congress has cataloged the hardcover edition as follows:
Cooper, Susan, 1935-
King of shadows / Susan Cooper.   p.   cm.
Summary: While in London as part of an all-boy acting company preparing to perform in a replica of the famous Globe Theater, Nat Field suddenly finds himself transported back to 1599 and performing in the original theater under the tutelage of Shakespeare himself.
ISBN: 0-689-82817-9 (hc.)
[1. Time travel—Fiction. 2. Actors and actresses—Fiction. 3. Globe Theater (Southwark, London, England)—Fiction. 4. Shakespeare, William, 1564-1616—Fiction.] I. Title.
PZ7.C7878Ki 1999 [Fic]—dc21   98-51127
ISBN: 0-689-84445-X (Aladdin pbk.)

For my actor

ONE

Tag. The little kids' game, plain ordinary old tag, that's what he had us playing. Even though none of us was younger than eleven, and the older ones were big as men. Gil Warmun even had a triangle of beard on his chin. Warmun was "it" for now, the tagger, chasing us; suddenly he swung around at me before I could dodge, and hit me on the shoulder.

"Nat!"

"Nat's it!"

"Go, go, go!"

Run around the big echoing space, sneakers squealing on the shiny floor; try to catch someone, anyone, any of the bodies twisting and diving out of my way. I paused in the middle, all of them dancing around me ready to dodge, breathless, laughing.

"Go, Nat! Keep it moving, don't let it drop! Tag, tag!"

That huge voice was ringing out from the end of the room, Arby's voice, deep as the sound of a big gong. You did whatever that voice said, *now;* you moved quick as lightning. For the Company of Boys, Arby was director, actor, teacher, boss man. I dashed across the room toward a swirling group of them, saw the carroty red head of little Eric Sawyer from Maine, chased him in and out and finally tagged him when he cannoned into a slower boy.

"Go, Eric, go—keep the energy up—"

The voice again, as Eric's scrawny legs scurried desperately through the noisy crowd; then suddenly a change, abrupt, commanding.

"O-*kay!* Stop! That's it! Now we're going to turn that energy inside, inside us—get in groups of five, all of you, anywhere in the room. I want small boys with small, bigger guys together, each group matching."

We milled about uncertainly. Small to medium, that was me. I linked up with two other boys from someplace in the South, a cheerful, wiry New York kid named Ferdie, and redheaded Eric, sticking to me as usual like a little shadow. Arby's big hand came down and removed Eric straightaway.

"Pick guys your own size, Sawyer." He replaced him with a bigger boy in unlaced high-tops and baggy jeans, with an odd face like a squishy pudding. I'd seen him around, but I didn't know him. Now there were four groups of five, and Eric left over. Arby put a consoling hand on his shoulder, and faced us all.

"Now cool it!" The voice boomed out, deep and hypnotic. He was holding Eric like a walking stick, like a prop; Arby was so completely an actor that sometimes you couldn't tell where the division was between performance and real life.

"This company is a family, a big family," he said. "Always remember that. We shall be performing in a foreign country, we shall be absolutely dependent on one another, we must each be *totally* trustworthy." He patted Eric absently on the shoulder, and Eric looked at his feet, embarrassed. But we were all listening, waiting.

Arby said, "The game you're going to play now is an exercise in trust. *Trust.* In each group I want one boy in the middle, the other four close round him."

The squishy-faced boy nudged me into the center of our group. I looked at him in surprise and he gave me an amiable, toothy grin.

"Each of you in the middle," Arby said, "shut your eyes, straighten your spine, turn yourself into a broomstick. Then fall, stiff, like a stick. Those of you round him, save him when he falls toward you, catch him gently, and gently push him toward someone else. Fall . . . and catch . . . fall . . . and catch . . . This is all about trust. The one falling must trust the catcher, the catcher must be trusted to catch. Go!"

I wasn't too sure I liked this game, but I shut my eyes and leaned to one side, falling stiff as a rail. I found myself against someone's chest, his hands touching my shoulders. For an instant my cheek was against his face, and then he was pushing me—I thought: *Stiff, stay stiff, Nat*—and like a pendulum I slanted toward the other side. And again hands stopped me, and gently shoved me back again.

So it went, like music in its rhythm, and it was fun. The feeling of giving yourself to other people, people you couldn't even see, flicked me back to being a very little kid, when my mother was still alive. I couldn't remember much about her, but I did remember how safe she made me feel.

The room was quiet; there was only the soft sound of hands brushing clothes, and feet shuffling a little, and a murmur of pleased surprise sometimes that must have come from the boys in the middle. Maybe from me. Arby's deep voice was a soothing background: "Fall . . . and catch . . . fall . . . and catch . . . Good, that's the way. Feel the trust . . ."

Then, falling, waiting for the reassuring hands to save me, I found myself not saved but still falling, and I shouted in alarm and stumbled, clutching for support, opening my eyes. I caught a look of mischievous glee on the face of the pudgy boy, as he grabbed me up just before I could hit the floor.

"Wow, sorry!" he said, grinning, mocking—and then his face crumpled into shock as a thunderbolt hit him.

"Out!" Arby was shouting. "You—out of this company! Go home!"

"It was just a joke," said Pudding-face, appalled. "I didn't mean—"

"You meant exactly what you did—playing your own little trick. We don't play tricks here, feller. *Nothing* is more important than the company, *nothing* is more important than the play. You betrayed a trust and I don't want you here. Out! Go pack your things!"

Pudding-face shambled out of the room, without a word. Someone told me afterwards that he was a wonderful actor; Arby had recruited him from a school in Cleveland, specially to play Bottom in *A Midsummer Night's Dream*. But back to Cleveland he went, the very next day. We never saw him again.

"Trust," Arby said softly, into the startled silence of the room. "Remember it. Someone else in the center, now. Keep going."

He pushed small Eric gently into the center of our

group, in spite of his size, and Eric gulped, closed his eyes and stiffened his back. The game went on.

There were twenty-four of us in the company altogether, if you counted Arby, his partner Julia, Maisie the stage manager, and Rachel the voice coach. The rest were all boys. The Company of Boys, chosen by Arby and his committee from schools and youth theaters all over the United States. We were all shapes and sizes and ages, up to eighteen. The only thing we had in common was that by accident or experience or both, we all knew how to act. Supposedly we were the best young stage actors in the country.

We had one other thing in common, too. Most of us were pretty weird. When you think about it, a normal kid wants to watch TV or movies, videos or computer games: there's something odd about him if instead he's more interested in the stage. And we were all crazy about it; crazy, and confident that we had talent. Arby had made sure of that when he first interviewed each of us, last winter.

Now it was summer. By bus or train or airplane, we'd all been brought to this school in Cambridge, Massachusetts, to rehearse two plays by Shakespeare together. Some rich theater nut had left money in his will to have Shakespeare's plays performed the way they were four hundred years ago, when he first wrote them. There were no actresses in the theater in those days; the women's parts were all played by boys whose voices hadn't broken yet. Some of the theater companies were made up of men and boys, some just of boys. Like ours.

And when we'd rehearsed for three weeks, the rich man's money was going to fly us across the Atlantic to

London, to perform at the new Globe, a theater that was an exact copy of the one the plays were first acted in, four centuries ago. We were going into a kind of time warp. My dad would have thought that was really cool: he was a big *Star Trek* fan. But I try not to think about my dad.

Arby called a break for lunch. That meant going down to the cafeteria of the school where we were working. Ferdie walked with me—not that he ever really walked, offstage; it was more a sort of spastic bouncing jive. He draped one arm briefly over my shoulders.

"That was *severe,* man. If he chops guys for little things like that, he's gonna have my ass in a week."

"I feel bad about it." I was remembering the horror on the pudgy boy's face, as Arby banished him.

"He could've hurt you," said little Eric self-righteously, shadowing me. "Could've broken your back, if you'd hit the ground."

"But he didn't let me hit the ground, he caught me. Just a bit late."

"Late is too late," said Gil Warmun, behind us. He towered over our heads as we all went down the stairs. "The old man was right—nobody can mess with trusting. You kids remember that."

"Okay, Dad," said Ferdie cheerfully.

"I mean it. You feel bad about that guy, Nat? That's dumb. He's history and he deserved it. Grow up."

"Grow up yourself," I said, stung.

Arby's big voice rang down the stairwell from above. The man was everywhere, like God.

"Read-through of the *Dream* in forty-five minutes,

gentlemen," the voice said. "And just bear in mind—this is going to be the most sublime six weeks of your lives, and the shittiest. In the theater, they go together."

The first weeks were certainly that kind of mixture. Even that first day. It wasn't literally the first day, because we'd had a rather muddled week of "orientation," but it was the beginning of serious rehearsal.

For the reading, Arby went on with his game pattern. He had us all sit cross-legged on the floor in a big circle, with our scripts, and he sat in the middle with a soccer ball in his hands. He threw his ball at each of us in turn, and when you caught it you had to say in a loud clear voice the name of the characters you were playing, then your own name and where you came from. Then everyone said hi to you. Then you threw the ball back. We'd been through this whole exercise once already, on the day we arrived, but I have to admit it was helpful to do it again.

The ball came at me, stinging my hand as I caught it.

"I'm Puck in *A Midsummer Night's Dream,* Pindarus in *Julius Caesar.* Nat Field, from Greenville, South Carolina."

It was Eric's turn.

"Eric Sawyer. From Camden, Maine. I'm Mustardseed in *A Midsummer Night's Dream,* and Cinna the Poet in *Julius Caesar.*"

We chorused, *"Hi, Eric!"*

"Character names first," Arby said. "They're more important than you are." Little Eric flushed. Arby threw the ball at the next boy, a tall, brawny character in a black tank top and black jeans.

"Duke Theseus in *A Midsummer Night's Dream,* Brutus in *Julius Caesar.*" He had a voice as strong as Arby's. "I'm Ray Danza from Chicago."

"*Hi, Ray!*"

The boy next to him was tall too, but chubbier, with a mop of curly black hair like a floppy Afro.

"Starveling in the *Dream,* Caesar in *Julius Caesar.* Hy Schwartz from Los Angeles."

"*Hi, Hy—*" and we all broke up, it sounded so silly. Everyone laughed except Arby.

"Get a haircut, Hy," he said, and he went on throwing the ball.

I was having a good time all afternoon until the middle of the read-through, when Arby lit into me for going too fast. He'd already told me twice to slow down, and I'd tried, but I guess I was nervous. We all were, of course. Everyone had a crystal-clear memory of the sudden end of Pudding-face's career.

It was in Act Three, when Puck has a long speech telling Oberon how his queen, Titania, has fallen in love with a donkey. Oberon is pissed at Titania because she's refused to let him have one of her servants, so while she's sleeping in a wood, he squeezes the juice of a magic plant on her eyes that'll make her totally obsessed with whatever person or creature she sees when she wakes up. (Oberon and Titania aren't human, they're the king and queen of the fairies—and if that makes you go "Haw-haw-haw," you might as well stop reading my story right now.)

I started out:

"My mistress with a monster is in love!
Near to her close and consecrated bower,
While she was in her dull and sleeping hour,
A crew of patches, rude mechanicals—"

"Puck!" Arby boomed from across the circle. "I keep telling you, will you slow down! We're acting this play in *England!* It's their language, it's called English—you can't help sounding like an American, but at least you can be *in-tel-li-gi-ble!*"

"Sorry," I said.

"A southern drawl has a certain charm," Arby said. Everyone was looking at him now. He smiled his famous warm smile at me, crinkling his eyes—and then suddenly the smile dropped away and his face was sour. It was as if a light had gone out. "But a southern gabble is hideous. Vile. You sound like a cross between a monkey and a duck."

There were some muffled sniggers around the circle. I wanted to disappear through the floor. From behind me a girl's calm voice said, "It's okay, Arby—we'll work on it, Nat and I. Hey—you chose these guys for their talent, not their accents."

It was Rachel Levin, and I could have hugged her. She was a student at the American Academy of Dramatic Arts, and she was attached to the company as Arby's assistant and our voice coach; I guess they felt we'd be able to relate to her because she was so young. They were right. I glanced around at her and she shook her long hair back over her shoulders and winked at me. The light glinted on the tiny diamond stud in the side of her nose.

Arby looked at her expressionlessly for a moment; I

was waiting for him to yell at her. Rachel looked calmly back. Suddenly he grabbed up his soccer ball, which was still beside him on the floor, and threw it violently right at her.

Rachel caught it, smooth as silk, though it rocked her backward. She smiled. "Voice coach and dragon's assistant," she said. "Rachel Levin, from Cambridge, Mass." She tossed the ball back to Arby, gently, and the rehearsal went on.

"He's so mean," Eric said. "He's mean to everyone. Is he always like that?"

Rachel was rummaging in her backpack. She laughed. "I don't think so. He lives with Julia, and she's quite the liberated lady." She produced a glossy green apple from the backpack, took a big noisy bite, and passed it on to Gil Warmun.

"Don't take it personally, Eric," Gil said. "Or you, Nat. He just wants everyone to know who's the boss." He bit into Rachel's apple and held it out to Eric. We were all sitting on the tired grass of the riverbank, beside the Charles River that flows slow and brown through Cambridge and Boston to the sea. Rachel had been hearing Gil and me do one of our Puck-Oberon scenes, and Eric was there because, well, because he was always there. It was a hot day, with only a whisper of breeze, and the air felt thick as a blanket. Joggers pounded by on the path a few yards away, glistening with sweat, and sometimes bicyclists whirred past them, perilously close. On the river, long slender boats zipped up and down, rowed by one oarsman or two, four or even eight; they were amazingly quiet, and you heard only the small smack of oars against water as the boats rushed by. Cambridge seemed to be a very competitive place.

I said, pointing, "Arby is like *that!*" A single oarsman was sculling furiously upriver, very close to our bank. As he came by you could see the intensity tight on his face, and hear the rhythmic gasps for breath.

"Obsessed," Gil said.

"Yeah."

"Nothing wrong with that, though. If he hadn't been obsessed with getting a boys' company to London, he wouldn't have got the money from that millionaire, and we wouldn't be going."

"It's not obsession," Rachel said. She reached out and took the apple back from Eric, who was already into his second bite. "Not like crew. I know people who row—if you want to be really good at *that,* it has to be like a religion. But theater? It's not a sport, it's not about winning, it's about people."

"And applause," Gil said, needling. "All those lovely hands clapping. That's what we all like most."

"Not true," Rachel said.

He grinned at her. "An actor's not much use without an audience."

"There you go then," said Rachel. "It's about people."

This wasn't a real argument though, it was cheerful bickering. We all knew Gil was as obsessed as anyone could be—in his case, with Shakespeare. He'd read every single one of the plays, and knew huge chunks of them by heart.

"What I like best is the *smell*, backstage," I said. I was thinking of the little theater back at home, where I'd played an evil little boy in a grown-up play last summer. It had been our space, my space, a kind of home. "Theater smell. Dusty. Safe."

"Good word," Gil said, sounding surprised. He reached out and gave me a quick pat on the shoulder.

"Safe," Rachel said thoughtfully. On the brown water, a pair of mallard ducks paddled slowly past us, and she threw one of them a piece of apple. The duck looked at her scornfully, and paddled on.

Eric said, "My mom thinks theater's *dangerous*. My dad had to talk her into letting me come."

Gil fingered his beard, looking at him deadpan. "She thought her beautiful little boy'd get attacked by nasty molesters? Not with that hair, kid."

Eric looked uncomfortable. "She's . . . religious."

"Arby had to do some convincing, with the younger boys' parents," Rachel said. "They couldn't understand why they couldn't go to London too."

"Why couldn't they?"

"This company is a family!" said Gil, in a perfect imitation of Arby's booming voice. "Families only have one set of parents!"

Eric looked at me. "Did yours care?"

"My what?"

"Your parents, did they get on your case?"

Oh please. I came here to get away from this. I thought I could get away from this.

I said, "I don't have any parents."

They all stared at me. Those faces stunned out of

movement for an instant, they always look the same. An eight slid past us on the river; I could hear the rhythmic creaking of the oarlocks, and the small splash of the oars.

"Oh, Nat, I'm sorry," Rachel said.

"I live with my aunt. She didn't mind me coming, she thought it was a great idea."

Don't ask me, please don't ask me.

Eric asked, direct, young, a hundred years younger than me: "Are they dead?"

"Yeah." I got to my feet, quicker than any of them could say anything else. "I gotta go pee—I'll see you back at the school."

And I was off, escaping, the way you always have to escape sooner or later if you don't want to be clucked over and sympathized with and have to listen to all that mush, or, worse, have to answer the next question and the next and the next. If you have to answer questions every time, how are you ever going to learn to forget?

It would be better in London, it would be better in the company; I wouldn't be Nat there, I would be Puck.

TWO

I loved London. It wasn't like any of the American cities I'd seen: Atlanta, New York, Boston, Cambridge. Looking down from the airplane, you saw a sprawling city of red roofs and grey stone, scattered with green trees, with the River Thames winding through the middle crisscrossed by bridge after bridge. When the bus first drove us in from the airport, everything seemed smaller than in the United States: the houses, so many of them joined together in long rows; the cars; the highways. There were tall office buildings, but not gigantic; there were super-markets, but not the same greedy sprawl. An English taxi-cab wasn't a regular yellow cab with a light glowing on the roof; it was a boxy black car whose shape dated back, Arby told us, to the days when it had to have enough room for a sitting-down passenger wearing a top hat.

Arby was full of stuff like that. He mellowed, the moment he looked down from the plane and saw all those lines and curves of little red-tiled roofs. He'd lived in England once, though nobody knew when or why he'd come to the United States, and somehow nobody had ever asked. Once he started talking to English people again, he began to sound a lot more English than he ever had at home.

Some of the Company of Boys stayed in a London University hostel north of the River Thames; some of us stayed in regular houses, each with a family. Most of these people were Friends of the Globe, members of a group who'd spent years helping to raise money to build the new Globe Theatre, the copy of the one where Shakespeare worked. My foster family was called Fisher. Aunt Jen had been nervous about letting me go stay with strange foreigners, until she had a long transatlantic telephone conversation with Mrs. Fisher and they both ended up swapping recipes for baking bread, which seemed to make her feel much better.

The Fishers lived in an apartment in a big ugly concrete block with a great view of the River Thames. There was a daughter, older than me, called Claire, and a son who was spending the summer doing a course at the Sorbonne, in Paris. I used his room. It had black wallpaper and several paintings of very strange, squashed-looking people, so I didn't ask too much about him. Claire was a serious girl whose favorite subject was politics, and she was always asking questions about the U.S. that I couldn't answer. She was very nice to me though; they all were. When I talked about living with my aunt, it didn't make them inquisitive, it made them keep their distance; like, oh, there's something private here, something we mustn't be nosy about. Maybe the Brits are all like that.

Instead of asking questions, the Fishers made sure they were even nicer to me. They had a flyer for our plays stuck up on their refrigerator door, and a poster out in the hallway to advertise us to the rest of the people in the apartment building. THE AMERICAN COMPANY OF BOYS, it said, with weird bright pictures of Bottom in his ass's head and Caesar with blood all over his toga. "We have tickets for both your opening nights!" said cozy Mrs. Fisher happily. "We're looking forward to it all so much!"

Mr. Fisher was a tall, bald man with a voice that rang out like Arby's, though he wasn't an actor; he worked in a bank. "But I've done a lot of amateur stuff, y'know," he said to me. "Trod the boards, after a fashion." There was a faintly apologetic note in his voice. Because we were to play at the Globe, and perhaps because we were foreign, he seemed to think of us as professionals even though we were only boys.

Gil Warmun was going to be a professional someday, that was for sure. The more I rehearsed, with him playing Oberon, the more I learned about Puck. I was a mischievous spirit but I was also a king's servant, and Gil never let me forget it. I ran lines with him every day before rehearsal, and had acrobatics lessons—they called it "tumbling"—with the other youngest boys, from an English friend of Arby's called Paddy, who had first been an Olympic gymnast and then worked in a circus. I was really happy. We all were. We thought about nothing but the two plays, and the day when we'd be up there performing them. Though we had classes every day, they were no more like school than chocolate cake is like rice pudding.

I had speech lessons often too, from Rachel, early in the morning at the house Arby and Julia had rented in Southwark, not far from the theater. It was a tall, narrow house made of brick, with a tiny front garden full of roses. I was amazed how many London houses had flowers on and around them, even if only in window boxes. Rachel lived in this house too, sharing a room with our stage manager Maisie, a quiet, chunky girl who knew how to yell like a drill sergeant.

Gil was there as well, in a tiny attic room at the top of the house. He and Rachel were a sort of couple, though they kidded around all the time. They'd each in turn been Arby's star pupil at the school where he taught drama, though Rachel must have been two years ahead of Gil. Next September he'd be joining her at drama school in New York. Someday I'm going to go there too.

I knew all my lines by now, and Gil's too.

> *"I am that merry wanderer of the night.*
> *I jest to Oberon, and make him smile—"*

Rachel said, "'Jest—to.' Two words, Nat." We were having an early rehearsal in the kitchen, while Julia answered phone calls in the living room. I guess you have a lot of phone calls to answer when you take twenty kids across the Atlantic for a month.

> "Okay. *I jest to Oberon, and make him smile*
> *When I a fat and bean-fed horse beguile,*
> *Neighing in likeness of a filly foal—"*

She turned her back to listen as I went to the end of the speech, and then held up a hand and turned around again. "It's good—the speed's just right now."

"And not too southern?"

"Nat—Arby knows as well as I do that you probably sound more the way they did in Shakespeare's time than anyone in this company. Or even any English actor."

I looked at her skeptically.

"It's true," she said. "The English and the Scots who settled those Carolina and Georgia mountains of yours, they took their accents with them. And because they didn't hear too much else up there, they didn't change, the way everyone else did." She turned to the sink and started rinsing the breakfast dishes.

"My gentle Puck," said Gil, "you're a fossil."

"Thanks a lot," I said.

"Maybe I should try to match him," he said to Rachel. He jumped up, spread his arms out to me and put on a heavy fake southern accent. "Ma jennel Perk, cerm hithah!"

"Poppa!" I said in a high falsetto, and flung my arms around his waist. Gil was a lot taller than me.

He laughed, rumpled my hair with one hand and shoved me away with the other. Rachel rolled her eyes, and closed the dishwasher. "Time out, comedians," she said. "You've got twenty minutes before rehearsal."

We were all a bit edgy, a bit silly, because today would be our first time on the stage. Everyone was looking forward to that. For a week now we'd been rehearsing in a school hall in Southwark, a tacky little place that was a temporary extension to a grade school, with little kids' drawings pinned up on fiberboard walls, and a smell of disinfectant. We had the outline of the Globe stage, and the two pillars we had to play around, marked on the floor with tape, but it was a poor substitute for the real thing. We'd had only a quick tour of the Globe so far; the regular adult company was playing there, and had needed the theater all day for rehearsals as well as performances. But now they'd opened their last production, and we could have the mornings.

Arby had decided we shouldn't see one of their performances yet, in case it influenced our own style. Gil and several of the older boys thought this was crazy, and intended to sneak off and watch, but Arby carefully kept us all working in the tacky school hall every afternoon—and the English company played in the afternoons, because that's what the original actors did, in the days before artificial light. (Today's company did 7:30 performances too, under lights designed to simulate daylight, but so far Arby had managed to keep all our evenings busy too.)

There was something really strange about Arby. He was such an intense guy, and yet sometimes he seemed to be coming from a great distance, as if he belonged to some other planet. He scared me a bit, when I first met him.

It was in Atlanta, and I was playing the small part of the Boy, in a Youth Theatre production of *Henry V.* Arby had come there on a recruiting trip for his Company of Boys, looking for actors good enough to come to his auditions. We all knew about those auditions; they were going to be held in New York two months later, for "boys between 11 and 18 with skills in acting, singing and acrobatics."

We were playing *Henry V* in a community theater, and we all shared one big dressing room. Arby came backstage to talk to the boy who was playing Henry, but he kept looking across at me, with those intent blue eyes, and pretty soon I found him next to me.

"You were the Boy," he said.

"Yes," I said cautiously.

"You were very good," he said. "Very good. What's your name?"

"Nathan Field," I said. "Nat."

And he laughed. It wasn't as if he thought my name was funny; it was a weird laugh, sort of triumphant.

"Yes," he said. "Yes, of course." The blue eyes were blazing at me; it gave me the chills. I could see a muscle twitching under his left eye. "Come to my auditions, Nat Field," he said, "come, or I'll be back to fetch you."

That stopped the chills, and anything else in my head; like all of us, I was longing to get into the Company of Boys. I said, "But on the application, it says 'skills in acting, singing and acrobatics'—and I'm not a great singer."

"You have the other two, so that doesn't matter," Arby said. "Doesn't matter at all. Not for my purposes."

He had the oddest look on his face, eager and crafty and mysterious all at once, and I couldn't figure it out at all. But of course I went to the auditions, with Aunt Jen, and he chose me to play Puck. And that was all that mattered to me. Or to Gil, or Eric, or Ferdie, or any of us in the company. *He'd chosen us*, to play at the Globe.

We ran through the grey London streets toward the theater. It was an awesome place; right on the River Thames, facing the banks of pillared granite buildings and glass office towers on the other side. They'd built it to look just as it had in Shakespeare's day; it was round, all white plaster and dark wood beams, with a real thatched roof made out of reeds, that ran in a circle around a gap. The middle of the building was open to the sky. It was a "wooden O"—that's what Shakespeare called it himself, in a speech in *Henry V.*

As we swung around the last corner, I stumbled and nearly fell. I guess I thought then that I'd tripped on a paving stone. For that moment, though, I had a strange giddy feeling, as if the buildings looming around me were moving, circling. My head was suddenly throbbing. I thought I heard a snatch of bright music, from some stringed instrument like a harp or a guitar, and I smelled flowers, the sweet scent of lilies, like in my aunt's garden—and right after it another scent that was not sweet at all but awful, disgusting, like a sewer. Was it real? I put my hand on the nearest wall, to steady myself, and Gil looked back at me.

"Nat? What's the matter?"

The buildings were still and safe again around my head. "Nothing."

I ran to catch up with them, and we hurried on. I said casually to Gil, "What a stink, at the corner there."

"Was there? I didn't notice."

But then we were at the theater, with Ferdie bopping along ahead of us toward the glass doors.

"Hey, Nat! How's your family, man—where you're living?"

"They're cool," I said. "I like them."

"I had oatmeal for breakfast, real thick and gooey, you could stand the spoon up. Porridge, they called it."

"Yuk."

"But with cream, and brown sugar. Turned out pretty good."

"A true artist, our Ferdie," said Gil. "Concerned with the really important cultural elements of life."

Ferdie didn't hear him. We'd just come through the last entrance into the theater, and the sun was blazing down through the wooden O of the roof, and there ahead of us was the great stage, five feet high.

"Wow!" Ferdie said.

We stood in the center of the theater, where the "groundlings" stood to watch the play—the people who couldn't afford to pay for seats. All around us, all around the almost-circle of the auditorium, the rows of seats reared up in galleries, way high, very steep, and in front of us the stage jutted out. It had two reddish marble pillars near the front—when you touched them, you found they were painted wood, but they sure looked like marble. They helped support a small roof covering part of the stage. If it rained during a performance, the groundlings would get wet, but the actors wouldn't. The underside of this roof was painted like a bright blue sky, with sun and moon and stars all up there together.

The long back wall of the stage had six small pillars set into it, echoes of the big ones out front, and three entrances, the central one a big space covered by a painted cloth, and the side ones two sets of big wooden doors. Above all this was a long stage balcony, where musicians played when they were needed.

Out onto the balcony, as we watched, stepped big Ray Danza, dressed in black as usual, as Theseus, Duke of Athens, and a slim fair boy called Joe Wilson, who was playing his about-to-be-duchess Hippolyta. Joe was about my age, and like all the boys playing women, he still had a husky-light voice.

Ray's strong voice rang out:

> *"Now, fair Hippolyta, our nuptial hour*
> *Draws on apace; four happy days bring in*
> *Another moon—"*

For a moment I felt giddy again; my head buzzed, as if the space were filled with voices. The air seemed hot, and again I could smell strange sour smells. I put out a hand for balance, and found myself grabbing Gil's arm. Jolted out of his focus on the stage, he mistook it for a nudge reminding him we should be onstage soon.

"Hey, yes, come on—I think it's this way—"

So we slipped out to find the way backstage, and into our first rehearsal at the Globe, and I forgot about everything else. It was wonderful. You could feel the play coming alive. I even found myself enjoying the parts between the four lovers—Lysander and Demetrius, two of Duke Theseus's courtiers, and their girlfriends Hermia and Helena—who spend most of the play wandering through a wood trying to figure out who's in love with who.

Then it was the turn of a bunch of workmen, real hicks, called Bottom, Quince, Flute, Snout, Snug, and Starveling, who plan to act a little play at the Duke's wedding feast. Bottom is the bossy one, he wants to play all the parts—and in real life, now that Pudding-face was out, Bottom was being played by a loud boy called David Roper, who was even more obnoxious than his character. I knew him a bit; he was the one who'd played Henry in the Atlanta production of *Henry V*, where I'd first met Arby. When he noticed my existence, which wasn't often, he called me Kid. From behind the back of the stage now I could hear him bellowing away out there—and I could hear Arby, from the first gallery where he was sitting, yelling at him to tone it down.

Then the "mechanicals," as Bottom and Company are called, came off and Puck and the Fairy were on, so out I ran onto the stage from behind the back curtain, turning two somersaults as I went, as Arby had planned it. I rolled to my feet, looked out at the theater—and was struck dumb. It was so amazing, being out in the middle of that rearing circle of gallery seats; it was so scary, it was so close.

I stood there with my mouth open.

"PUCK!" roared Arby.

I jumped, saw little Eric frowning at me onstage, and nearly died of shame. *"How now, spirit!"* I said feebly. *"Whither wander you?"*

"GO BACK!" came the deep voice. "DO IT AGAIN! Wake UP, Nat!"

This time it was perfect; I came up from the second somersault just as Eric, running, reached his mark, and we were facing each other and zipping into the lines.

"How now, spirit! Whither wander you?"

Eric came close, as if to tell me a secret.

"Over hill, over dale,
Thorough bush, thorough briar,
Over park, over pale,
Thorough flood, thorough fire,
I do wander everywhere. . . ."

Eric onstage was a different animal from meek, shy little Eric in real life. His face was alight with excitement, his voice clear and high as a flute; he was this eerie little creature the Fairy, flickering about to serve Titania, his Queen. We darted through our short scene, telling about the row between his mistress Titania and my master Oberon:

"—but room, Fairy! Here comes Oberon!"
"And here my mistress! Would that he were gone!"

And from either side of the stage came Gil as Oberon with his gang of magic attendants, and the amazing-looking boy who was playing Titania, Alan Wong, who had an ageless, perfect face that might have made you think him a real sissy, if you hadn't known he was already a karate brown belt at the age of eleven.

"Ill met by moonlight, proud Titania—"

Even without costume or makeup Gil looked like a real king, with his back straight and his head held high. Eric and I had to hang out, each of us behind one of the big stage pillars, while Titania and Oberon argued about the boy servant they both wanted—until Titania went away, cross and obstinate, with Eric scurrying after, and I was left with Gil.

"My gentle Puck, come hither—"

—and he went on with his speech with one hand cupped around the back of my head, just the way my dad sometimes used to hold me. I got goose bumps from the feel of it. That's a short scene, Oberon sending Puck off to find a magic herb with which he's going to bewitch Titania (and Demetrius and Lysander too, as it turns out) as a revenge. I darted across the stage at the end:

"I'll put a girdle round about the earth
In forty minutes—"

Arby boomed out from in front: "Nat! Can you jump off the stage on that line without killing yourself? And exit through the house?"

I looked. It wasn't that much of a drop, and I had a good run-up. "Sure."

"Do it."

"I'll put a girdle round about the earth (run)
In forty minutes—" (leap)

—and I was soaring over the edge and down to the groundlings' floor, landing with bent legs, staggering a bit, running for the exit.

"Arby!" Gil was at the edge of the stage, calling out, concerned. I turned back to listen. "Arby—he can't do that with an audience there—he'll kill someone! He'll hurt himself!"

There was complete silence in the theater for a moment, a dangerous silence. Then Arby said, very quietly, "Warmun, I am directing this play, for this century, and you will all do exactly what I tell you."

It was a weird thing to say, but there was absolute authority in his voice. Nobody said anything.

"It's your cue, Oberon," Arby said.

So Gil went on with the scene, until the point where Demetrius comes on, pursued by unlucky Helena (who loves him), ungratefully trying to get rid of her as he hunts the eloping Hermia (whom he loves) and Lysander. And I went backstage to wait for my next entrance.

It's Puck who causes most of the trouble in *A Midsummer Night's Dream*. After Oberon has squeezed his magic herb's juice on Titania's sleeping eyes, so that she will fall in love with the first thing she sees when she wakes, Puck finds the mechanicals rehearsing their play in the wood, and changes Bottom's head into a donkey's head. Bottom's friends run away, terrified—and guess who Titania first sees when she wakes?

Oberon has seen Demetrius being mean to Helena, and felt sorry for her, so he tells Puck to squeeze the magic juice on *his* eyes too, so that he'll switch from Hermia to Helena. Unfortunately Puck mistakes Lysander for Demetrius, and instead of sorting out the lovers he makes things worse. Pretty soon neither girl has the right guy in love with her, each of them is mad at the other, and the men are threatening to kill one another.

I had a great time leading each guy about the stage in the dark, putting on a deep voice to make him think I was the other one—until at last by the end of Act Three, which Arby had chosen as the place for our intermission, all four lovers were asleep and things could be sorted out by having Lysander fall back in love with Hermia.

I said, squeezing the juice on his eyelids:

> *"When thou wak'st*
> *Thou tak'st*
> *True delight*
> *In the sight*
> *Of thy former lady's eye;*
> *And the country proverb known,*
> *That every man should take his own,*
> *In your waking shall be shown:*
> *Jack shall have Jill,*
> *Nought shall go ill.*

> *The man shall have his mare again,*
> *and all shall be well."*

And these last three lines I said out to the audience, or rather to the empty theater where the audience would be, and they jarred me suddenly out of my happy time, my acting time. *All shall be well.* I knew as I said it that it was a lie, Shakespeare's lie, because I knew from my own life that all does not go well, but that terrible things happen to people and cannot be put right, by magic flower-juice or by anything else in this world.

As I stood there on the stage, for the third time that day there was the weird blurring around me, as if I were underwater, and a buzzing in my head like the voices of a crowd, and through it a faint thread of music. The stage pillars and the galleries beyond them seemed to tilt and sway, and I felt myself stagger.

"Nat?" said Arby's voice from out front, inquiringly.

Gil must have been watching me from behind the up-stage curtain, because suddenly he was out on the stage, holding me by the shoulders, looking down into my face in concern. "What's wrong, kid? Are you okay?"

"Sure," I said. And sure, yes, I was okay, for as long as the play would last. Until I got back to real life, where nothing could ever really be okay again.

Gil and Rachel walked me back to the Fishers' that afternoon, even though the giddiness was gone again in minutes, just as it had been before. Everyone seemed to be treating me like some fragile piece of china, even Arby—though I guess that was understandable because he didn't want anything to happen to his Puck. Eric was my understudy, and his voice projection was better than his tumbling.

I felt healthy enough, all through supper with Mr. and Mrs. Fisher and Claire; I even had a second helping of shepherd's pie, my favorite discovery about British food. But afterward, as we watched a series on television that always made the Fishers fall about laughing, I began to feel sick to my stomach, and slipped out to the bathroom just in time to throw up.

Claire was on her way to use the bathroom just as I was coming out. She stared at me. "Are you all right, Nat? You're white as a sheet."

"I lost my dinner," I said. I tried to grin. "It was so good—what a waste."

I went into my room and sat on the bed. I felt very cold suddenly; I was shaking all over. Claire must have gone straight back to her mother, because in a few moments Mrs. Fisher was beside me, her arm around my shuddering shoulders, her hand on my forehead.

"It wasn't the shepherd's pie," I said miserably.

"It's that twenty-four-hour virus that's going round, I reckon. Were you sick? And diarrhea?" I nodded, and she gave me a brisk hug. "Poor Nat. Into bed with you—I'll get something to warm you up."

By the time she came back, I was curled up in bed in my pajamas. She'd brought a hot drink that she made me sip cautiously—hot lemon with some sort of medicine in it—and one of those floppy English hot-water bottles, made of rubber covered with a fuzzy woolly fabric. I cuddled it to me, like a little boy with a warm teddy bear. My head was throbbing. I felt really sick, and about four years old.

Mrs. Fisher felt my head again gently. "Try to sleep," she said. "I'll check you again in a little bit. You'll feel better in the morning, I promise."

She pulled the curtains to shut out the daylight, which lasts longer on English summer days than it does where I come from, and I guess she went away, but that's all I remember of that night. There's only darkness when I try to look back, and the feeling of being sick, and the buzzing in my head.

But I'll never, ever, forget the next morning.

THREE

Between night and morning, Nathan Field has a dream, a dream of flying.

He flies high, high up, in the dream, up into the stratosphere, out into space. Space is dark, and prickled all over with bright stars. Then he slows down, coasting and turning in space, as if he were swimming underwater; and below him he sees the planet Earth, bright in the darkness, spinning like a blue ball.

He hangs there for a moment, and then he feels a hand take his own. He can see nobody, there is simply the feel of the hand. It holds him firmly, and pulls, and following the pull he dives down, toward the blue planet. It grows larger and brighter, and he can begin to make out the patterning of oceans and continents. Down he goes, down, until he is heading into a white overlay of clouds.

The hand draws him on, on, into the next day.

FOUR

"Nat?" said the voice. It was a young voice, sort of husky, and it had an accent I didn't recognize: halfway English, halfway American. "Nat?"

"Unh." I woke up with my face in the pillow, and even before I opened my eyes I knew something was wrong. My face and my body told me that I was lying on a different pillow, and a different bed; hard, both of them, and crackly. The bed was really uncomfortable. I moved my hip; surely it wasn't even a bed, but a mattress on the floor.

Maybe I was dreaming. Blurry with sleep, I turned my head, blinking in the daylight, and saw looking down at me the face of a boy I'd never seen before. He had long curly dark hair down to his shoulders, and black eyes, and he looked worried.

"How do you?" he said. "Is your fever less?" He reached out a cautious hand and felt my forehead.

I stared at him. "Who are you?" I said.

"Harry, of course. Harry, your new fellow. Have your wits gone, Nat?" He peered at me. "You look—strange, a little. Thin in the face. But better. Dear Lord, I was afraid you had the plague."

I lay very still, with all my senses telling me that I had

gone mad. *The plague? Nobody's had the plague for centuries.* Everything was different. This was a straw mattress I was lying on; I could feel bits of stalk prickling through the cover now. My pajamas had gone; I seemed to be wearing a long shirt instead. The room around me was smaller, with one window, divided into small panes. Sunlight slanted in through it to show rough plaster walls, a threadbare carpet on the floor, and a smaller one draped over a sort of bureau. I grew aware gradually of a rattle and hum of voices and creaking wheels and the chirp of birds from outside the window, and a stale smell in the room like . . . like something I had smelled before, but I couldn't think what, or when.

I was baffled, and frightened, though at least I didn't feel ill anymore.

I pushed back the rough blanket over me and scrambled to my feet. The shirt reached to my knees. My head reeled, and the boy Harry saw that I was shaky and reached for my arm. I realized that I needed to go to the bathroom. I said: "I have to—"

He smiled, understanding, looking relieved. "Tha must be better if tha needs a piss," he said, and he drew me to a corner of the room and took a flat wooden cover off a wooden bucket, whose smell made it instantly clear what it was for. I stared at it blankly, but Harry had turned away to fold up my blanket, and since there was no time to argue, I went ahead and used the bucket. It had been pretty well used already, for assorted purposes. When I'd finished, Harry came over, glanced outdoors, picked up the bucket, and in one shatteringly casual movement, emptied it out of the window.

Such a small thing, such a huge meaning. I guess that was the moment when I first began to think, with a hollow fear in my chest, that I might have gone back in time. It was like being in a bad dream, but the dream was real. The night into which I had fallen asleep had sucked me down into the past, and brought me waking into another London, a London hundreds of years ago.

I leaned weakly against the wall. "Where am I?" I said.

Harry put down his reeking bucket and grabbed my shoulders, hard. He stared nervously into my face. *"Art thou he they call Robin Goodfellow?"* he said.

I said automatically, *"I am that merry wanderer of the night."*

"Thank the good Lord," Harry said, looking relieved. "At least thou hast thy lines." He moved me sideways and then downward, to make me sit. So there I was, sitting on a little stool topped with a hard cushion, sitting in a century long, long before I was born.

"Th'art Nathan Field," he said, looking me deliberately in the eye, speaking slowly as if to someone deaf or half-witted. "Come to our new Globe Theatre for a week from St. Paul's Boys, since we lost our Puck for Master Shakespeare's *Midsummer Night's Dream.* Th'art a wonderful actor, they do say, though it seems to me too much learning at that school has addled thy wits. Unless the fever has done it. Tha joined us yesterday, remember? We rehearsed lines, just thou and I together."

How could I say: *Yes, I remember?* That wasn't what I remembered at all.

"Aah," I said. *Our new Globe Theatre,* he had said. In 1999, where I lived, it was the Globe's four hundredth anniversary. So, if the Globe was new, this was 1599.

I sat there gaping at him, trying to cope with the unbelievable, with being bang in the middle of something that was totally impossible. All I could think was: *Why is this happening to me?*

"Come," Harry said. "It's past five. Master Burbage will be up and ready—dress, quickly—" And he began thrusting clothes at me from a heap at the bottom of the mattress; it was lucky he was there, to show me the right order. There was a kind of padded jockstrap of thick rough cotton; then long dark tights, like those I'd worn onstage sometimes but much worse fitting; then a bulgy, padded pair of shorts, a thin floppy undershirt, and a fitted jacket to match the shorts. A doublet, he called it. Around my waist went a leather belt, with a knife like a dagger in a leather sheath attached to it.

"And I cleaned thy shoes," Harry said, and held them out; they were leather, rather like loafers, with a buckle on top. "Tha couldst never have done it, the way tha wast last night."

"Thank you," I said.

I have to write down the way he spoke, the way they all spoke, not as they really sounded but as I understood them. I'll use things like "thou" and "tha" for "you," sometimes, just to remind you that they didn't sound like us, but I can't make you hear the real speech. It was like a thick, thick dialect, with strange vowels, strange words, strange elaborate phrases. But it was more like the speech of my home than the English of today's London or New York, so perhaps that's how I understood them and they understood me.

Or then again it could just be part of the whole

impossible change that took me there. I was living, but not in real life at all.

A round-faced woman came in, kind looking, with a long dress, a white pleated ruff around her neck and a sort of floppy cap on her head. Harry said at once, happily, "See, Mistress Burbage—he's well again."

She took my chin in one hand and felt my forehead with the other. I had the best-felt forehead in London by now, it seemed to me. "The Lord be praised," she said, and then she looked at me critically, reached to the bureau, and took a damp cloth and scrubbed my face with it. I laughed, feebly, and she gave me an amiable pat. She reminded me of my Aunt Jen, a little; she was a link with the real world, in this mad dream that I was living.

Down a wooden staircase we went, clattering, Harry leading; it wasn't much more than a slanted ladder, with a rail to hold on to. In the room below, a man was sitting at a heavy wooden table with plates and mugs in front of him, and a sheaf of papers; he was chewing, and muttering to himself through the mouthfuls.

"Good day, Master Burbage," Harry said, so I said it too, and Burbage blinked at me. He was a chunky, good-looking man, younger than Arby, older than Gil. He had a neat beard, and a rather big nose. His doublet was a wonderful glowing blue, with a broad collar.

"Better, art t'a? Good!" he said, and went back to his munching and muttering.

Mistress Burbage filled two mugs for us, from a jug with a curly handle; all these were made from a grey metal that I found out later was pewter. There was a big round loaf on the table, and a hunk of white cheese, both on square wooden plates. Harry cut us slabs from both of them, with his knife. Suddenly hungry, I took a big bite, chewed, and washed it down with a swig from my mug. The drink was cool, sour tasting but not unpleasant; I realized, with a shock, that it was a kind of beer. Ale, they called it, and it was the main thing I drank in all my time there; a weak homemade ale was the main thing everybody drank, from morning till night. You could say the whole population of Elizabethan England was slightly buzzed all day long.

Burbage said to himself, through his bread and cheese, *"If I were fair, Thisbe, I were only thine. . . ."*

So he was learning Bottom's part. I knew that bit. Bottom the Weaver comes back onstage saying his lines for the little play they're rehearsing, and his buddies rush away screaming because Puck has given him an ass's head.

I said, very fast and agitated, *"O monstrous! O strange! We are haunted! Pray masters, fly masters! Help!"*

Burbage chewed more slowly, looking at me. I could see a muscle twitching in his cheek, under his left eye. It looked sinister, though later I realized that it was just a sign of mild stress. "Hast played Quince too?" he said.

"Puck is onstage for those lines," I said.

"Thy memory is good. Will Kempe says thy tumbling is even better, is that true?"

"I do well enough," I said modestly, thinking: *Wait till I show you.* I knew that Arby had put me in the company partly because of my cartwheels and somersaults, back flips and handstands. For the way he wanted to do the play, they were as important as my acting or singing.

But I wasn't working for Arby now.

I had no time to worry about that; Burbage rushed us through our breakfast, eager to get to the theater. "Across the bridge today," he said. "No boat. We need to use our legs."

He swung a wonderful short cloak about his shoulders, the same blue as his doublet, and Harry jammed a flat floppy hat on my head and the same on his own. Master Burbage had a hat with a brim, and a curling, slightly battered feather. He wore it at a jaunty angle. Out we went, raising the wooden latch of the heavy front door.

And their London swept over me, caught me up, in a nightmare mix of sight and sound and smell. Even before six in the morning, the street was filled with people bustling about, carrying huge bundles, selling fruit or pastries or pamphlets from trays slung from their necks, dodging to avoid men or horses. Carts clattered over the cobbles, creaking, rocking, splashing up muck sometimes from the stinking ditches into which Harry and everyone else had emptied their waste. Water ran through those ditches, but slowly. There were flies buzzing everywhere. The whole street smelled bad; so did the people sometimes, if a particularly unwashed one jostled you too close. Where there were gaps in the crowd, squawking crows and ravens hopped and pecked and fought over garbage in the ditches.

We passed shop fronts where bloody meat hung on enormous hooks, or vegetables and fruit were set out in gleaming rows, or a wonderful smell of fresh bread wafted out from hidden ovens. We passed a door with a bush tied over it, and the stale smell of ale strong from inside, and raucous shouting. We stayed close to Master Burbage,

Harry and I, as he strode lordly down the street with his hand on the hilt of his short sword. People greeted him, here and there; sometimes he lifted his plumed hat, but he never paused. I scurried along in a blur of amazement, wonder and the beginnings of fear, past delights and horrors. A dog with no ears or tail snapped at me beside a bank of glorious roses set out for sale, and a beggar clutched at me, screaming, a filthy child with no legs, propped on a little wheeled trolley.

Then we were around another corner into an even more crowded street, narrow, lined with tall wooden buildings; between them I caught glimpses of the flat brown River Thames. We were crossing the river; the street was the bridge. It was London Bridge, I found out later; the only way of crossing the river except by taking a boat. There were houses built all along it, a row on either side, their roofs touching over the road running between. It didn't take us long to cross over; the Thames was not wide here.

And above the roofs where the bridge ended was the worst horror of all: a series of tall poles, with a strange round lump stuck on the top of each, lumps that gleamed white here and there, lumps attracting flurries of crows and other black birds that shrieked and tore at them, pecking and ripping and gobbling. It was only when I saw the farthest pole topped by a grinning white skull that I realized all the round lumps were human heads, the heads of men and women chopped off by an axe, and I stopped abruptly and heaved up my breakfast into the reeking ditch.

It occurred to me later that I'd now thrown up in two

different centuries in the space of twenty-four hours.

Harry patted my back, consoling me over this last sign of my departed fever. Master Burbage was only concerned in case I'd splashed my tights.

FIVE

In the Fishers' concrete apartment block overlooking the River Thames, the boy Nat lies shivering in bed, curled up, clasping his hot-water bottle, growing gradually warm. He sleeps a little.

Then he grows warmer, hotter, his fever rising; he tosses off the bedclothes, muttering, sweating, no longer knowing who or where he is. Mrs. Fisher comes back to check him. Flushed and damp-skinned, he is barely recognizable. Alarmed, she tries to wake him, but the fever is galloping, edging on delirium. She has never seen anything like this. His skin is on fire, his hair wet with perspiration; there are strange swellings in his neck. She calls her husband, and in sudden fear they telephone their doctor.

The doctor is not at home. They call for an ambulance. It takes the boy to Guy's Hospital: a short swift ride through the dark midnight streets. In the emergency ward, nurses receive the boy in puzzled alarm; they start sponging down the fevered body, they peer at the red swollen glands. Meningitis? The doctor on duty comes, frowns, orders an intravenous line, blood tests, antibiotics. Surprising the nurses, he orders the boy to be moved to an isolation ward. Intent, unsmiling, he goes to an office where there is a telephone with a direct outside line, and he closes the door. He calls, even at this hour of 3 A.M., a colleague who is a specialist in tropical medicine.

He says, "You aren't going to believe this, but I think we have a case of bubonic plague."

SIX

"There it is—our new theater!" said Harry proudly. "Hast seen it before?"

"No," I said truthfully, staring. A white flag was flying from the flagpole on top of the Globe, the signal to audiences that a play would be done there that day. For the moment, it was the only thing I recognized. It wasn't the theater itself that was so startlingly different from the copy that would be built in my time; it was the surroundings. This Globe wasn't crowded and dwarfed by towering office buildings; it stood up proud and high, and to the south it looked out over green fields and billowing trees. In fact there were trees nearly all around it; once we had left the main street that went over London Bridge, I'd felt, with astonishment, that we were walking into the countryside. The streets were still busy and noisy, though, with carts and coaches and horsemen, and others like us bustling on foot.

Like the Globe of my own time, the theater looked new; its plaster gleamed white, the reeds of its thatch lay tight and straight-edged. As Harry chattered proudly on, the apprentice of the Lord Chamberlain's Men explaining his company to the borrowed boy from St. Paul's School, I realized that it really was new, finished only a few

months earlier. Before that, the company had been playing for years in a theater—called, believe it or not, just
The Theatre—across the river, in Shoreditch, until their
lease on the land ran out and the landlord refused to
renew it. Master Burbage and his brother Cuthbert had
just inherited The Theatre from their father, James, who
built it. There it stood, useless, on ground they weren't
allowed to set foot on. Where were they to act?

It was the actors who solved the problem, Harry said,
grinning. Five of them got together with the Burbages,
raised enough money to lease a piece of land here in
Southwark, and hired a master carpenter. ("My uncle,"
said Harry possessively. "His name is Peter Streete.")
Then, one dark winter's night just after Christmas, taking
a dozen strong workmen with them, they went quietly to
Shoreditch and with axes and sledgehammers and crow-
bars they took The Theatre apart. They did it very carefully, numbering each piece, and it took them three days.
The demolition must have been a very noisy process, but
Harry said not many people lived in the area close by.

After that they carted all The Theatre's major beams
and timbers to the River Thames—huge oak beams, Harry
said, some of them thirty feet long—and shipped them
over to the other side. And there, using them for a frame-
work, Peter Streete and his workmen gradually built the
theater that they christened the Globe.

Birds were singing in the trees outside the theater as
we went in. The doors seemed smaller than in my day,
and in different places, so that I couldn't tell whether
we were headed backstage or for the groundlings' pit. I
followed Harry and Burbage blindly, through narrow pas-

sages, past busy preoccupied men and boys; the whole theater had an odd musty, grassy smell that I couldn't place, and everywhere of course there were the unfamiliar accents and clothes. To keep from thinking I was crazy, I'd begun to pretend that I was in the middle of a movie set in Elizabethan times, among actors dressed in costume. It was comforting until something screamingly real hit me, like those heads over London Bridge.

Two boys hurried past us, paused, and looked back, calling to Harry. I went quickly on after Master Burbage, who was climbing a narrow staircase. From somewhere beyond it came the sound of voices, indistinct but loud, one of them very loud, as if angry.

There was bright light ahead of us all at once. Master Burbage paused, and I found we had come out onto the central little balcony at the back of the stage. I had to step over a coil of thick rope lying on the balcony floor, and saw one end of it tied firmly to the balcony rail; it was a knotted climbing rope for a quick descent to the stage, something Arby had planned to use in my own time. I might have thought myself still in my own time if it hadn't been for Master Burbage at my side. Ahead and around us were the empty galleries of the theater; above us the painted sky of the "heavens" that gave the stage its roof—and below, on the broad thrusting stage, two figures, arguing. One of them—a small, lean, brown-faced man—was pacing angrily to and fro, thumping his fist into the palm of his other hand.

"Thou shalt never have me back!" he snapped at the other man. "I shall dance my nine days' Morris, I shall be the wonder of London, and who will come see thy clowns then, I'd like to know! Lose Will Kempe and you lose his following—and then you will all be sorry!"

"Indeed thou hast a great following, Will," said the other man mildly. He was sitting on a stool at the front of the stage, with a book at his feet.

Will Kempe wasn't listening. "And I shall write the tale of it!" he shouted. "My own book, I shall write! Th'art not the only wordsmith in this company, only a great fusser and fiddler who would have every point his own!"

"I tie no points," said the man sitting down. "I guard only the words I set down." I liked his voice; it was soft, but pitched to carry. Without ranting and raving, he was just as forceful as this small angry man. I liked his face too, lined and humorous above the short brown beard. It wasn't an old face, but one that had seen a lot.

He stood up, and held out his hand to the other. "Play our *Dream* once more, Will," he said, coaxingly. "Play once more, before a great lady."

"'Tis a dream of your own," Will Kempe said coldly. "She will not come. And I am gone, and you and Dick may go hang."

He swung himself over the edge of the stage, with the nimbleness of an acrobat, and marched across the floor of the yard—a dirt floor, where two men, oblivious of the shouting and the fury, were raking up a layer of some sort of coarse grass. Out he went, out of the theater. The man below us sighed.

Over our heads, doves were cooing in the thatched roof, a long burbling sound.

Master Burbage called down, "I told thee! I told thee! So now I am thy Bottom, heaven help me."

The bearded face tilted up to us. "Thou art my top and my bottom and all things between, Dick Burbage, saving decency." His eyes were a strange color, a dark tawny mixture of hazel and green. They shifted toward me. "Is this the boy?"

"Will Kempe's lad, who will not now be playing with Will Kempe." He poked me in the back. "Greet Master Shakespeare, boy."

Shakespeare. *William Shakespeare.*

It was as if he'd said, "Say hello to God."

I stared down at the stage, speechless. I suppose we were ten feet or so above him. For a moment I couldn't move—and then more than anything I wanted to be closer to him. On impulse I grabbed up the climbing rope and tossed it over the rail; then swung my legs over and went down it, hand over hand, feet gripping the rope. Fortunately he was far enough forward that I didn't kick him in the head.

My feet hit the stage. Harry had jammed my cap so firmly on my head that it was still there, so I pulled it off and ducked my head in what I hoped was a neat little bow, the way Arby had taught us.

Will Shakespeare grinned at me. He wasn't a tall man: he was about Gil's size. His hair was receding, leaving lots of forehead, like in the pictures you see in books, but he didn't otherwise look much like the pictures at all. There were more lines on his skin, lines from laughing, and a thicker beard. He wore a little gold hoop in his left ear.

"So you are Nathan Field." The hazel eyes were looking me over, appraisingly.

I said rather shakily, "They call me Nat."

"Well, Nat, welcome to the Chamberlain's Men. Thy friend Will Kempe has left us in a huff—wilt play in our company even now he is gone?"

"Oh yes!" I said instantly. The words must have come out so fast, so eager, that both Shakespeare and Burbage laughed.

"When he was my friend he spoke highly of thy tumbling," Shakespeare said. "And Dick Mulcaster of thy voice, bless his generous soul. We have all whirled you about London this past day or two, Nat—do you understand what's happening?"

This was so on the nose that for a dizzy moment I thought he must know where I really came from, who I really was. "No, sir," I said.

But he didn't know. He said, "Three days from now we are to play a piece of mine from some years past, *A Midsummer Night's Dream*. We had more boys in the company when first we played it—now we have only enough for the women, and we lack a boy for Robin Goodfellow, for the Puck. So Richard Mulcaster, having played the play of late, has of his kindness lent us his Puck. You."

I wished I could ask him who Richard Mulcaster was. "I know the lines," I said.

"Ah. He says thou hast the memory of a homing pigeon. Who knows, I may keep thee." He smiled his quick smile, to show he was joking. "We had no love for the Paul's Boys when we were playing on your side of the river, but Dick is a friend of mine from long ago. A wise, gentle man. And a gentleman too."

"Yes," I said. Down in the pit, the two men had finished their raking and were starting to untie and scatter new bundles—of what I now saw was not grass but a thicker green stem. Reeds, I guess. They gave off the odd smell that I'd noticed all through the theater; they made a kind of disposable carpet.

"'Ware heads, below," said Master Burbage from above, and he swung himself over the edge of the gallery and shinnied down the climbing rope fast and expertly, with his blue cloak billowing out behind him.

Shakespeare shook his head. "The man is all actor," he said.

"And a good thing for you," said Burbage, "considering he plays four parts this week, all large." He looked down at me, suddenly serious, and glanced out at the reed scatterers, as if to make sure they couldn't hear him. He said quietly, almost in a whisper, "Nat Field—one thing I will tell thee that Master Shakespeare has not, since th'art living in my house and will hear more than tha should. Our *Dream* is revived so suddenly not by choice, but by command. The Queen wishes it. She has a fancy to see our sweet new theater, but will have us play nothing in it for her but that."

"But this must not be breathed to a soul," Shakespeare said. "She will come in secret. Bankside is not Blackfriars, and these are dangerous times."

Burbage took hold of one of my ears, not gently. "Mention it to anyone and I will cut off thine ear," he said. "Very slowly, inch by inch."

I thought of the heads stuck on poles, and decided he might mean it. "I promise," I said.

Will Shakespeare moved back to the stool and picked up his book. It was not a printed book, I saw, but a bound manuscript. He glanced up at the sky over the pit; sunshine was starting to slant down over the edge of the hollow roof. "Time passes," he said. "This wooden O of ours is a sundial. Classes, Richard."

I looked at the lines on his face, and at his ordinary brown doublet and hose, and I thought: *Don't go, please don't go.* It wasn't because he was William Shakespeare. I just knew that I liked being with him, more than with anyone I knew.

He moved away, then looked back at me. "We shall rehearse together soon, Puck," he said. "I am to play thine Oberon."

More than anything from that first day, I remember the noise. You'd think that we have more noise today in the everyday world, what with traffic and airplanes and so many different kinds of machines that didn't exist then, not to mention radio and TV and cassette players. But the London of that time was full of church clocks striking the quarter-hours, and church bells ringing for services; of watchmen ringing handbells in the street and shouting out the time, and town criers calling out the news. Everyone who sold anything shouted out his or her wares. People have always been noisy, I guess, in towns at any rate. At the Globe Theatre, nobody ever seemed to speak softly if he could shout.

"Nathan Field! Where's Nathan Field!"

It was a very large voice from a very small man; small but fat, dressed all in light grey. He looked like a button mushroom, and he was marching onto the stage from the tiring-house, the dressing space behind it, with a group of five boys straggling behind him. One of them was Harry.

"Here he is," said Master Burbage. "And the space is thine for half an hour, Henry—no more." He clapped the mushroom on the back and headed for one of the upstage exits. Over his shoulder he said, "Master Condell is here to tie thee in knots, Nat."

One or two of the boys sniggered. Master Burbage disappeared through the door. Small stout Henry Condell looked me over critically. "Well, Nathan Field," he said, "we shall see what a Paul's Boy has to offer us. This precious half hour is tumbling practice. I will not turn thee into a show. Just try to follow what the others do."

"If you can," said one of the boys cockily. He was about my age but smaller; dark haired, very wiry and agile looking. I guessed he was probably the star gymnast. Henry Condell glanced at him with something close to dislike.

"Go first then, Roper," he said. "Somersaults."

Roper did a quick sequence of somersaults across the stage, light as a feather. The others followed him, one by one; two of them, Nick and Alex, were quite good, Harry was so-so; the last, a chubby, fair-haired boy called Thomas, was a real klutz. He rolled sideways out of his second somersault, and giggled. Master Condell sighed.

"Follow, Nathan," he said.

Head over heels over head over heels I went across the stage, faster than Roper, ending with a jump. I was better than any of them; but then, somersaults are easy.

The boys watched me in silence, warily.

"Cartwheels," said Master Condell.

One by one we cartwheeled back toward him; Harry turned two, the others three, Roper and I four. Thomas tried to turn one cartwheel and ended in a hopeless heap. This bothered him not at all, and the others seemed to take it for granted, but Roper snorted in disdain. He opened his mouth to say something, caught Master Condell's eye, and shut it again.

"Walk on your hands," said Henry Condell.

Roper and I made it across the stage; Nick and Alex fell down halfway. Thomas couldn't get up onto his hands at all.

"Forgive me, Master Condell," he said cheerfully. "If I practice for a year, I shall still have no balance."

"You never practice at all," Roper said.

"Each man has his own talents," Henry Condell said mildly. "Now—I want to see the display you have each devised for me in these last three days. I expect to be gratified, surprised, and dazzled. Or at the least, pleased."

Thomas said, "May I be first?"

Master Condell blinked. "You surprise me already. Very well—let us give Thomas the stage."

He hopped over the edge into the groundlings' yard, with startling agility for someone so round, and we followed him. Thomas stood up on the stage looking pudgy and lumpish, and very woeful. For the next few minutes the sad expression on his face never changed, but he went through a mimed routine that was so funny it had every one of us, even Roper, helpless with laughter. He was playing himself, the hopelessly incompetent gymnast; he went through a huge effort to complete each movement, failing more and more disastrously each time. His longing to succeed was so achingly apparent, and his failure so ludicrous, that it broke your heart while you laughed and laughed. He was a natural clown, of a kind I've never seen before or since, and he was brilliant.

Henry Condell said, wiping his eyes, "Thomas, I thank thee. Thine apprenticeship will never be damaged by thy tumbling."

That was the start of my gradually realizing that each of the boy actors in the company called the Lord Chamberlain's Men was an apprentice, learning his craft. Unlike the boys who were being trained in schools—the real Nathan Field, for instance—they were out in the real world very young, learning to act by doing it. The adult actors were their teachers, and each boy was apprenticed to a particular one of the adults. Harry was Master Burbage's apprentice, which was why he was living in the Burbage house.

Thomas ducked his head mournfully to Master Condell, still with his sad clown's expression, then caught my eye and flashed me a quick grin.

Each of the boys in turn got up on the stage after that and went through his own little tumbling routine: a mixture of required movements and personal tricks put together to be as showy as possible. If they'd had parallel bars or a vaulting horse, it would have been like watching mini-versions of Olympic routines. They were all pretty good, even Harry, who seemed to have fairly inflexible joints, but Roper was by far the best. He turned cartwheels and back flips and leapt about the stage as if he were made of rubber, and ended with a double flip that brought out a gruff "Bravo!" from Henry Condell.

Roper jumped lightly down from the stage and landed at my side. I said impulsively, "That was great!"

He looked at me with a twisted little smile that had no pleasure in it, just malice. Nobody had ever taught this boy how to like other people. "Now do better, Paul's Boy," he said nastily, and he sat down cross-legged on the ground.

What he didn't know was that I could in fact do better. I'd been good at gymnastics ever since I was very young; the phys ed teacher at my little grade school in Greenville had been a passionate gymnast and tai chi expert, and I'd been his prótegé, even after I'd gone on to junior high. We'd worked out a real show-off routine that had been the high point of my audition in front of Arby, when I was trying out for the Company of Boys. Four hundred years from now.

Henry Condell shook his head, frowning. "This is not a contest," he said. "Nathan has not worked on a display."

"But there's something I can do," I said. "May I?"

Roper laughed.

Master Condell's eyes flickered from one to the other of us. He didn't really like this situation; he was a kind man. "Very well," he said.

So I got up on the stage, ungracefully, and I took a deep breath and I did my routine. It started with a double flip from standing, and it went on through some really phenomenal stuff, some of it made out of tai chi movements, to end with a triple back flip that I only just managed, because of having been sick. I wobbled a bit but I landed standing, hearing them gasp, and there was a tiny silence and then all the boys clapped. So did Master Condell.

But not Roper. He just sat there.

Henry Condell said to me, *"Who taught thee?"*

I searched for a name Will Shakespeare had used. "Master Mulcaster," I said.

Condell's eyebrows went up, and he looked at me with extreme skepticism. I looked back innocently, and he frowned uncertainly, and shook his head. "Richard Mulcaster's tastes must have changed since last I had words with him," he said.

I suddenly remembered the other name. "And Will Kempe," I said.

Condell's face cleared, and he laughed. "I had forgot thy connection," he said. "Angry Will, who has stalked out, I hear, leaving me to find the money to buy his share in the company. Thy cousin, was he?"

"Will Kempe was Nat's mother's cousin," Harry said importantly. I had found him suddenly at my side after I did my show-off turn, though he hadn't paid me too much attention before that.

I said, "I have not seen him often this past year." That was certainly true.

"He taught thee well," Condell said. He was looking at me thoughtfully; I hoped he wasn't going to ask about the tai chi.

Inside the back of the theater, someone was ringing a handbell. Roper scrambled to his feet. "Our time is over, Master Condell." For our different reasons, he and I were both glad of the interruption.

The boy actors often had classes in the morning, I discovered—taught by whichever member of the company was free and willing. After the tumbling class, Master Burbage came back and gave us a lesson in what the others seemed to call declamation, though I'd have described it just as verse speaking. Everyone had a prepared speech that they got up and delivered from the stage. Burbage went up to the very top gallery of the audience, and bellowed down criticisms from there. The worst crime was to be inaudible, though it seemed to me that most of the boys were trying too hard to be heard, and overacting horribly as a result. Master Burbage seemed to think so too. "Not so much!" he would yell down at them. "Not so much!"

I didn't recognize most of the speeches they did. They were pretty ranty and ravy, and I don't think any of them was from Shakespeare. When it was my turn, I wanted to do the "To be or not to be" soliloquy from *Hamlet,* which I'd learned for my audition for Arby, but it occurred to me just in time that I didn't know whether Shakespeare had written *Hamlet* yet, in 1599.

I didn't want to do a speech of Puck's in case they thought that was the only thing in the world I knew by heart, so I did Oberon's speech, when he's telling Puck what they're going to do with the juice of the magic flower that makes people fall in love with whatever they see. It starts:

> *"I know a bank where the wild thyme blows,*
> *Where oxlips and the nodding violet grows. . . ."*

I was so nervous that I did all the things Arby hates: I went much too fast, and I sounded like a real southern boy from the Carolinas, not at all like an Englishman.

While I was rattling along I saw a movement up in the gallery, as someone joined Master Burbage; I couldn't see who it was and I didn't care. I was just relieved when I got to the end of the speech without forgetting the words. But when I'd finished, a voice came soft but clear from up there, echoing through the theater, and it wasn't Richard Burbage.

"Well done."

It was Will Shakespeare.

He didn't stay. He went away again almost at once, and before long it was another class, given this time by a quiet, serious man called John Heminges. Fencing, he taught us. That is to say, he divided us into pairs and he watched us fight. We wore masks for protection, thank goodness, and we used rapiers, longer and heavier than any I'd ever seen, with a kind of button on the tip to keep you from hurting or being hurt.

I fought Harry first. It was kind of a joke, because I've done hardly any fencing; I just know the basic moves. And this kind of fencing was different; you didn't parry a sword thrust, you jumped out of its way, or ducked, or knocked it aside with your left hand, on which you wore a very heavy leather glove. Harry realized how little I knew as soon as we started, and was very patient; he never pushed me, but if we'd been fighting for real, I'd have been dead in the first half-minute.

Then we changed partners and I got Roper.

He was as good at fencing as he was at gymnastics, and twice as aggressive. He wasn't about to be patient with my clumsiness; he was going to make me look as bad as he possibly could, to get his own back. He yelled in triumph every time his rapier touched me, which was every few seconds, and he chased me all the way around the stage, stabbing and lunging as I backed helplessly off.

"Let be, Roper!" Master Heminges called at last. "This is the Paul's Boy, is it not? He has not thy training."

"No—nor any skill neither," Roper said nastily. And his rapier came full at my throat, and would have hurt, button or no button, if John Heminges had not grabbed his sword arm with a large strong hand and twisted it roughly.

Roper yelped with pain and his rapier clattered to the floor, and I knew I had a real enemy now.

SEVEN

By the time fencing class ended, my stomach was growling loudly to tell me that it was lunchtime, though I didn't ask about that—which was just as well since I guess the word *lunch* wasn't used much in the sixteenth century. They ate midday dinner, anywhere between 10 A.M. and 2 P.M., and it was the main meal of the day. For us this time it was a kind of picnic, to be eaten fast before starting work at the theater. The plays were put on at 2 P.M. every afternoon, close to the times they would be done four hundred years hence in the theater designed to be a copy of this one, and if you weren't acting, you'd be working backstage.

Mr. Heminges gave a few pennies to a bigger boy who'd just joined us, Sam Gilbourne, who was the senior apprentice, and he herded us outside and bought street food from a girl with a tray around her neck. It smelled wonderful. We each got a kind of turnover, a big pocket of tough pastry with meat and potatoes inside, and a wooden mug of ale from another street seller, a one-legged man with a barrel on a cart. Sam had six mugs with him in a bag; they were pretty clunky, and smelled of stale beer, but I was thirsty enough not to care. If you didn't bring your own mug, you had to drink right there from one of the communal cups that were attached by a leather thong to the handle of the ale seller's cart.

The noise outdoors was stupendous, even an hour before the play was due to begin. The air was filled with voices shouting and calling, the rumble of wheels, the whinnying of horses, and over it all the shrill cries of the hawkers selling food and drink. The streets around the theater were crammed with people, and here and there tumblers and musicians working their hearts out for an odd coin. It was more like a fairground than a city street.

We ate our pies, as Sam called them, perched on a fence over the river, watching long low boats called wherries unloading passengers at a jetty near the theater. Two or four brawny men rowed each boat, with long heavy wooden oars. Bigger boats, with sails, tacked up and down the river; it was much busier than in my day, and much more open, because there were hardly any bridges. London Bridge was the only one in sight.

Sam was a friendly, almost fatherly boy. You could tell from the huskiness of his voice and his gangly arms and legs that he was going to be too old to play women's parts pretty soon. But he was to play one this afternoon, in a play called *The Devil's Revenge,* in which his character had her throat cut halfway through.

"Pig's blood," he said cheerfully, chewing a piece of gristly meat. "To be squeezed from a bladder in my sleeve. And a beating if even a spot of it lands on my skirt."

Roper snorted. "And show me a real throat-cutting where the blood does not splash everywhere like a broken waterpipe."

"No matter," said Sam peaceably. "The groundlings

are happy so long as they see it gush. Come, we must go back." He tossed his piece of gristle into the air, and three screaming seagulls made a dive for it. And I ran back to the theater, trying to keep up with the group, wondering uneasily where and how Roper had seen a man's—or a woman's—throat cut.

The Devil's Revenge was full of blood and murders, and a spectacular swordfight, and from behind the stage you could hear the groundlings who stood in the yard yelling with delight. It made great use of a trapdoor in the center of the stage, through which the Devil carried people off to Hell, and I was given the job of helping chubby Thomas open and shut the trap, down in the dark space under the stage. Roper was our signalman, standing a few yards off in a place where he could peer through a gap at what was happening onstage. He would make a chopping motion with his hand when it was time for us to knock aside the heavy wooden latch that kept the trapdoor closed.

We'd been shown what to do by a tireman, a wizened, grey-haired little guy who grinned a lot, even though he was missing most of his front teeth. Strictly speaking his job was looking after the wardrobe ("tire" means "attire" means "costumes," I found out), but he seemed to me more like a stage manager. He took us to the "plot," the list of the play's actions and exits and entrances that hung on the wall backstage, for everyone to check what they should be doing next. There were three trapdoor drops in the course of the play, and the cues for each were marked.

The first two went well; we couldn't always hear the words above us clearly, through the wood of the stage and

.the noise of the audience, but Roper's signals gave us our cue. Each time, Master Burbage, playing the Devil, came dropping down through the trap clutching another actor, and both of them landed lightly on their feet, on the big padded cushion that was there on the floor just in case. Burbage caught my eye the second time, and grinned at me, a startling fantastical grin in the elaborate makeup that slanted his eyebrows up and out.

But the third time, nobody was grinning.

I didn't understand what went wrong, at the time. We knew the cue for the third drop was almost due, and we were watching Roper carefully for the signal. I was closer to him than Thomas, and probably blocking Thomas's view. So I was the one who saw Roper's arm come smartly down in the same swift chopping motion as before, and I hissed to Thomas, *"Now!"* We knocked aside the latch and the trap dropped open—and through it, in a whirl of arms and legs, tumbled Master Burbage, taken by surprise. He fell on his back, and if it hadn't been for the cushion he might have been badly hurt.

We heard a great roar of laughter go up from the audience, who had seen the Devil, in the middle of a highly dramatic speech, suddenly fall through the floor, and we saw Richard Burbage's face change from astonishment to furious rage. He caught me a whack around the side of the head with his open hand, and aimed another at Thomas, who managed to duck. "Half-wit dolts!" he yelled at us over the uproar from the theater, and he rushed angrily out.

Then just for an instant, in the dim light of that darkened space, I caught the tail end of a satisfied smirk on

Roper's face that told me he had deliberately signaled us to do the wrong thing.

*　*　*

He denied it completely, of course.

"You waved at us!" I said indignantly. "You waved at us just the way you had before."

"I did no such thing," Roper said coolly. "Thomas, did you see me wave?"

Thomas looked at me, troubled, but he was an honest fellow. "No, I did not," he said. "I was too close to Nat—but I know he saw something, he was so definite."

"He was mistaken," Roper said. He gave a patronizing little sigh. "His ignorance made him nervous. They are a soft lot, in the boys' companies."

I was on the edge of punching him, but Sam's large hand was on my shoulder. He said mildly, "Thou hast been known to make a mistake, Roper. So have we all."

"Not such a stupid mistake as this, to ruin a whole play," Roper said.

"Enough!" Sam said sharply. "The thing is over, and paid for." After the play, Master Burbage had been angry enough to beat us, and I knew it was only the fact that I was on loan, and not a regular apprentice, that saved Thomas and me from a thrashing. But the tongue-lashing he gave us had almost been worse.

"He will still be angry at the house tonight," Harry said ruefully. "There will be no supper for you, Nat, and likely not me neither."

Roper said, "Enough. Let's go to the bear pit. There's time."

We were sitting under a tree near the theater, all six of us. The adult actors had all gone their ways, some to their homes, some to an alehouse. Round-faced Henry Condell had emptied a bag of apples into our hands as he left. He had heard Master Burbage's rage, and had looked at me sympathetically, I thought. The apples were small and a bit worm-infested, but crunchy and wonderfully sweet.

"Time but no money," Harry said.

"Thou needst none. I have found a way in. Come." Roper glanced at me maliciously. "Unless your Paul's Boy has no stomach for it, of course."

So of course I had to go with them. Through the crowds, through streets that grew narrower and noisier, full of rougher trade, jostling and cursing. It was the kind of area where you kept a cautious hand on your purse, if you had a purse. Loud, quarrelsome men lurched out of alehouses; women in low-cut dresses leaned out of windows and called softly, or not so softly—indeed some of them came stumbling out into the streets, calling, clutching at men's sleeves. Harry and the rest shouted catcalls at them, and dodged their pinching fingers. Trying to follow Sam, I came face-to-face with one of them, a woman whose dress hung half open, torn. She was not much more than a girl, but her teeth were blackened and uneven, and her breath in my face stunk of garlic and ale and decay. There was an open sore on her cheek, and her eyes were empty, without any expression. She was probably not much older than me. She was gone in an instant as we rushed by, but I can still see that face in my mind.

The bear pit was like a theater, a little; it had the same

shape, it had the same outer wall, the same shouting audience. There were two entrances, with gatherers to take your penny fee. Roper hustled us past them to a place halfway around the building where there was a reeking pile of garbage.

"Hold your noses," he said, and he pulled back a loose piece of wood in the wall, close behind the garbage, and one by one we slipped through, into the bellowing crowd. Nobody noticed. We came out under a ledge that was a bit like the space underneath the bleachers at a baseball field. Galleries ran all around the walls, like a theater, but the focus of the bear pit was a central arena, fenced in, with people standing all around.

We were moving through people so excited they never glanced at us; in the din and confusion it was hard to know what words they were shouting. Screaming, some of them, men and women alike. Harry tugged me into a gap, and I looked out into the arena and saw what they were screaming about.

In the center of the space, a huge brown bear was tethered by a chain to a heavy wooden post. The chain came from a collar around his neck; it was maybe four feet long. Around him, leaping up, snapping, snarling, barking, were three smooth-haired dogs as big as wolves. I couldn't tell what breeds they were, but they were awesome muscular creatures, one black, two brown. Teeth bared, they flung themselves at the bear in furious intent to kill. With wordless, bloodthirsty shouts, the crowd urged them on.

The bear was bellowing, striking out with his powerful forearms; his mouth was open, and foam dripped from his long yellow teeth. In one long swipe he hit the black dog, and his sharp claws opened the animal's belly like a knife. The dog screamed. You could see its guts begin to spill out as the body spun sideways to the ground. The crowd shrieked with delight, or horror, or both, and I looked away, feeling sick. Around me the other boys were yelling with the rest.

I had to look back. Two men were dragging the black dog's twitching body away. Another dog was released into the arena, smaller, chunky as a pit bull; it too rushed at the bear, but silently, teeth bared in a soundless snarl—and suddenly the three dogs seemed to start working instinctively as a team. The first two leapt at the bear from one side, turn by turn, twisting in midair to avoid the flashing claws, and while the bear's head was turned, straining against the collar and chain, the third dog jumped for his throat.

The crowd roared. Even over the din you could hear the bear bellow with pain and rage. His face was turned full in our direction as he tossed up his head, blood dripping from his neck, and in sick horror I realized that he could not see.

I shouted into Harry's ear, appalled, "The bear is blind!"

Harry's cheerful open face was alight with excitement. "Of course—Blind Edward—they put out his eyes, for better sport." He shouted in sudden glee. "Look there!"

In his blind fury the bear had swung with all his force at the smallest dog, or where he supposed the dog to be, and had chanced to hit it full on, sideways. The animal was dashed to the hard ground, lying instantly still, and whether from a slash or a ruptured artery, blood poured out from its body in a bright pool.

. . . *blood on the floor, bright red, a pool of red blood, spreading* . . .

"No!" I said, choking, caught inside my memory. "No!" And I flung myself away from the other boys, stumbling as blind as the bear, pushing my way through the crowd to find the gap in the wall, and the stinking pile of garbage that was less sickening than the joy of the people in that shouting crowd.

EIGHT

For three days the time went by with much the same pattern to each day: classes or rehearsal in the morning, work during the performance; an hour or two with the other apprentices before supper and bed. Most of it was like a nightmare. Roper had decided to turn my life into a misery, and he made the most of every smallest chance. Because I was such a misfit, there were plenty of them.

There was hardly a moment when I wasn't aware that I didn't belong. I suppose a lot of it was what they call culture shock: the business of suddenly finding yourself without all the little everyday goodies that a kid living in the twentieth century takes for granted. Not only all the people and places of my life were missing but all the support systems too: electricity, gas, plumbing, running water, refrigeration, central heating, regular plates and knives and forks, packaged food, canned food, paper tissues, toilet paper . . . Without any of those, living in 1599 was like being on a permanent camping trip in a third world country. I began to feel grubby all the time, and itchy, and hungry, and vaguely sick.

At night, it was hard to sleep. Harry would lie on his mattress beside me, dead to the world, breathing evenly and peacefully, while I lay lost in my miserable thoughts, missing my own world, fighting off panic. What had happened to me, and why, and how? Where was the real Nathan Field? If I'd traveled through some sort of time warp, how was I going to I get back again?

What was everyone doing about my disappearance— Gil, Rachel and Arby, and Aunt Jen way over there at home in South Carolina? Had they told Aunt Jen? Did they think I was dead? A voice wailed in my head like the voice of a very small boy: *I want to go home . . . I want to go home . . .*

I didn't let myself cry, because the last time I cried was when my father died, and that was something not to be thought about, not ever. Instead I'd lie there listening to all the little sounds of the Elizabethan night: the small outdoor shrieks of animals or birds, the rustling indoor sounds that might be rats or mice or cockroaches. I wouldn't fall properly asleep until the first faint glimmer of dawn, and then there were very few hours left before the early beginning of our day.

The other boys, I began to realize, thought that my oddness was the result of my background, Nathan Field's background. As Roper liked to remind me, I was a St. Paul's Boy, a sheltered, educated softie from the choir school, where you performed plays only once or twice a week, in a swanky indoor playhouse for rich highborn folk. If my accent was different from theirs, my diction or training or vocabulary, they knew it was because I hadn't been thrown out into the world at the age of ten and apprenticed to a company of actors.

Even my everyday clothes, I belatedly noticed, were better than theirs. I was privileged, living here only as a loan, and I would shortly go back to my privilege. (Would I really? Was I to have to cope with a whole separate new life again soon, at St. Paul's School? I fought off panic at the thought of it.) Roper's principal reason for his extreme dislike of me was simple envy.

But I didn't feel privileged or enviable. I'd never been more miserable in my life.

Roper made a great story out of my reaction to the bearbaiting, and told it to anyone who would listen. He buttonholed two of the younger actors, Bryan and Phillips, one morning, as Harry, Thomas and I were sweeping the stage with twig brooms before rehearsal. Roper was supposed to be sweeping too, but he stood twirling his broom, reciting his tale with malicious glee while the actors smiled indulgently. He had begun to refer to me as "the little lass," which filled me with fury.

"So the bear pulls the guts out of Ned Ashley's dog— tha knows? the big black hound?—and the little lass looks a bit green, she closes her eyes. Then she *really* has a fainting fit when Quayle's terrier has its head smashed open. 'No!' she calls out"—he put on a high, ridiculous falsetto—"'No!'—and she runs away with her petticoats all abuzz—"

"Leave me alone, Roper!" I said angrily, as the actors chuckled. I wanted to bash him with my broom, and he saw it. He swung his own broom up into the air, holding it out like a barrier with one hand at either end.

"Quarterstaves, is it?" he said, and he came at me, pushing me with the flat of the stick, nudging me to the edge of the stage.

"Hit him, Nat!" said Thomas indignantly. "Pack him

off!" And I was on the verge of doing just that, which of course was just what Roper wanted, when one of the actors, Bryan, strolled languidly across the stage, and then suddenly, startlingly, drew his dagger and held it straight out between us.

"Good actors do not quarrel," he said. He didn't look at me, but I think he was feeling bad about having laughed.

"And brooms are for sweeping," said a deeper voice, behind him.

Everyone turned to look. It was Will Shakespeare, just come onstage from the tiring-house.

Roper wilted, in immediate respect. Bryan put his dagger away. Shakespeare's eyes flickered from one to the other of us, and he chose to keep things light rather than heavy. "By your leave, good sirs, I need the stage for half an hour," he said. "I also need a Puck without a broken head."

They were gone before you could see them go; they all evaporated, like early mist. Will Shakespeare smiled at me, moving to stage center, and without another word he went straight into our first scene together in *A Midsummer Night's Dream*, after Titania has had her fight with Oberon and left in a huff.

> *"Well, go thy way; thou shalt not from this grove*
> *Till I torment thee for this injury.*
> *My gentle Puck, come hither—"*

He beckoned me. Instinctively I obeyed the direction that Arby would give me four hundred years from now, and I went to him in a double somersault. I came up on my feet close enough for him to touch me. Shakespeare, surprised, laughed aloud. He made no comment, he just went on.

> "—*thou remember'st*
> *Since once I sat upon a promontory,*
> *And heard a mermaid, on a dolphin's back,*
> *Uttering such dulcet and harmonious breath,*
> *That the rude sea grew civil at her song,*
> *And certain stars shot madly from their spheres,*
> *To hear the sea-maid's music?"*

"*I remember,*" I said. Puck doesn't have too much to say in this scene. Master Shakespeare went into Oberon's speech about the magic flower that he wants fetched ("love-in-idleness," which he told me later was another name for a pansy) and sent me off to find it.

> "*Fetch me this herb, and be thou here again*
> *Ere the leviathan can swim a league.*"

I was hopping around him like a bird longing to fly.

> "*I'll put a girdle round about the earth*
> *In forty minutes—*"

That was my exit line. I remembered Arby's direction, and I paused, uncertainly. "Can I go off through the house?"

"Through the house?" Shakespeare said.

I pointed into the auditorium.

"No, no," he said firmly. "That is for clowns, and not clowns of my liking. Thy place is the stage."

"Tumbling, then?"

"Show me."

I threw myself hand over hand and cartwheeled across the stage toward the exit door. Arby had worked this out too, for a different scene, and I knew it looked good from the front. Shakespeare chuckled.

"Very pretty," he said. "I have a dancing Puck. Yes— and let thy tumbling carry thee right off the stage and out of sight. Find a trusty door opener, to save thy head."

"Yes!" I said happily.

"Do not choose young Roper," he said, and smiled wryly when he saw me blink. "Oh, Nat," he said. "This company is a family, close and closeted. We all know what that miserable boy is at, and I am sorry for it, and for thee. But he is talented, and useful, and apprenticed to my friend Heminges—canst forgive us thy troubles, for the play's sake?"

He put his arm over my shoulders and gave me a quick hug. And to my absolute horror, I fell apart. It was the sudden warmth and sympathy, the fact that somebody understood—and not just anybody, but *him*. I heard myself give a great ugly snorting sob, and suddenly, hating it, I was in a flood of tears.

Will Shakespeare was astonished, and probably appalled. By accident, he'd released an emotional overload far bigger than he expected—and far bigger than I could ever explain to him. Not that he gave a thought to explanation; he sat down abruptly on the stage, pulling me down with him, and sat there with his back against the great wooden pillar while I sobbed into his shoulder. He didn't try to stop me; he just waited, patting me gently, saying softly once in a while, like a mother to a very small child, "There. There now."

In a little while he said quietly, "There is more here than persecution by a nasty boy. What ails thee, Nat? What is it, this terrible buried sorrow? Dost miss thy parents?—where are they?"

How did he know, to go to it so fast and direct, through four hundred years? He thought he was coping with lonely Nathan Field of 1599, but his instinct took him ahead through centuries, to a truth that he couldn't possibly have sensed. Like an arrow he went to my haunting, which I had tried so hard and so long to hide from everyone, and most of all from myself. With a small innocent question, he made me dig myself out of a grave.

I lifted my head off his damp sleeve and looked out at the groundlings' yard, though I wasn't seeing it. "She died when I was five," I said. "She had cancer. She was very pretty and she smelled of flowers, and she used to sing to me. But she died, and that left my dad and me, just the two of us. My Aunt Jen—she's his sister—she came to live with us, to help, and after a while things got better, I thought. Dad would play games with me, and I'd help him in the garden. He liked his garden, he had rosebushes for Mom."

Will Shakespeare was sitting absolutely still, listening, waiting.

"My dad—" I said, and I had to swallow, to keep going. "My dad missed her. I was all he had left, and I tried to be enough for him, but I wasn't. I wasn't enough. He went on missing her. One day I came home from school early. And he was lying on the floor of his study, he'd killed himself. He had all her old letters around him, there was blood on the floor, bright red, a pool of red blood, spreading." I had to swallow again. I could see it all so clearly.

Shakespeare shifted a little. He said quietly, "Nat Field. Thou hast a lot to bear."

Suddenly I wanted to defend my father. "He didn't mean me to find him," I said. "He'd locked the door and left a note for Aunt Jen, with the key. He just didn't know there was a spare key." I felt another sob come welling up like a huge bubble. I tried to stop it, but it came out as an ugly croak.

Will Shakespeare sat there with his hand on the back of my neck, rubbing it gently. "I have seen men die," he said. "Too often, and always for bad reasons. But here is thy father dying for love of a woman, and that is even harder to bear, especially for his son. I had a son—" He stopped.

I said, "Had?"

"He died, three years ago. He was just your age. A sweet pretty boy."

I said, "I'm sorry."

"Thy loss was the greater," Shakespeare said. "I have two daughters still, one of them his twin."

"What was his name?"

"Hamnet."

I said, thinking I'd heard it wrong, "Hamlet?"

"Hamnet," Shakespeare said. "He was named for my oldest friend, and my daughter Judith for his wife." He turned his head and looked at me oddly. "What dost thou know of Hamlet?"

"Only the name," I said.

"I have a new play in mind, for Burbage—" But he was looking at my face more closely, and I guess he saw it was still all covered in tears and snot. He pulled a cream-colored handkerchief from a slit in his sleeve, and mopped me up. Then he took hold of my chin to make me look him in the eye, straight and serious.

"Listen to me," he said. "Do not say thou wast not enough for thy father. Never say that. Some things are beyond our command. A man so caught and held—men will destroy much for love, even the lives of their children, even their own lives. I have a poem that I shall copy for thee, that thou shalt read and remember. *Remember.*"

He jumped to his feet and called out, to an invisible Helena leaving the stage:

> *"Fare thee well, nymph; ere he do leave this grove*
> *Thou shalt fly him, and he shall seek thy love."*

It was my next cue for coming onstage. I sniffed hard, took a deep breath, and stood up, facing him.

He said: *"Hast thou the flower there? Welcome, wanderer."*

I held out an imaginary pansy. *"Aye, there it is."*

Shakespeare smiled. *"—I prithee, give it me.*
I know a bank where the wild thyme blows. . . ."

And on we went, into the rest of our scenes together, until one of the tiremen came looking for him to put him into his costume, because soon the day's play would begin and he had a part in it.

Shakespeare tugged at his beard, exasperated. "We are but halfway through our scenes, and two days hence is the *Dream,* with this our untried Puck—"

"And thirty minutes hence is Master Jonson's play," said the tireman unsympathetically, "and thou not yet in reach of thy costume."

I pulled back the curtain at the back of the stage to let them into the tiring-house, which was buzzing with actors and musicians. Master Burbage was there, painting a spectacular depraved makeup onto the chubby face of Thomas, who was to play an elderly whore. Shakespeare was still lost in his own head as the tireman, clicking his tongue like an anxious mother, began unbuttoning his doublet. "Richard," Shakespeare said to Burbage, "a thought—let us have the boy's things taken from thy lodging to mine, since time is so short. Breakfast and supper may give me the space to run lines with him."

"Hold this," said Burbage, thrusting a dish of purple paint into my hands. He dipped in a brush, and began painting the closed lids of Thomas's eyes. "Lord love you, Will, you'd think there were no other play toward in London but this little *Dream* of thine. Nat, canst tolerate living in the house of a mad poet for a few days?"

"Oh yes sir," I said. "I think so."

NINE

Isolated in Guy's Hospital, the boy Nathan lies half-conscious in bed, his head tossing from side to side on the pillow. His wrists are tied to the bed by padded restraints because he has twice pulled the intravenous line out of his arm, and that line—carrying fluids, nutrients, and antibiotic drugs—is the only thing keeping him from death. The nurses are not troubled by the unfamiliarity of his face, because they have never seen him before; nor by his strange ramblings and cries of fear, because he is semidelirious and cannot be expected to behave like a normal boy. They are concerned only with the astonishing fact that he is suffering from bubonic plague, once known as the Black Death, and that he must, if possible, be cured.

Chubby Nurse Stevens, who has just been sponging the boy's thin, fevered body as best she can, pulls a sheet over him and rests a gentle hand briefly against his cheek. Nathan opens his eyes and stares up at her, distraught; he can see only her brown eyes, in the dark face covered by the white mask. The eyes crinkle, as she smiles at him behind the mask, and without really thinking about it, she hums him the tune she was singing last night in St. Anne's Parish Hall, at a rehearsal of the early music group that is her only recreation.

Lullay lullay, my littel tiny child. . . .

It's a pretty tune—a carol, really. In the sixteenth century, mothers used to sing it to their babies. Nathan's head stops tossing. His eyes gradually close, and he falls asleep.

TEN

So I found myself living in the house where Will Shakespeare lodged, and where, for the time being, he wrote his plays and his poems. He spent hours at a time sitting in an upstairs room, scratching away with a quill pen, beside a window that looked out onto a crab apple tree. The pen must have driven him crazy; he had to trim it often with a special little sharp knife, and a bristling bunch of big new feathers sat on his desk waiting for the moment when he threw the old quill irritably on the floor and reached to sharpen a new one. I longed to be able to hand him a ballpoint pen.

He was up there in his room my first day, when Harry and I brought my clothes from Master Burbage's house, and the woman who looked after him, Mistress Fawcett, wouldn't let us go upstairs. She was a fat, friendly soul, and gave us each a handful of little sugary cookies as consolation.

"Nobody must disturb him when he's writing," she said reverently. "But in any case thou art to sleep down here, Nathan—the room behind the kitchen. Too warm for summer, perhaps, but cozy."

Harry was deeply impressed by my room, which wasn't much bigger than a closet. It was the bed that did it: a little wooden bed, not unlike the one I had at home, four hundred years and three thousand miles from here. "A jointed bedstead!" he said, big-eyed. "And sheets, look! And a pillow!"

Mistress Fawcett had smiled proudly. Her house was quieter than Master Burbage's, even though it was in a busier area; it was set back from the road and had a walled garden behind it that Master Shakespeare's room and mine both faced. The streets all around were hopping, though. This was a district called a "liberty," free from all the rules and regulations that had to be obeyed in the proper City of London across the river. Will Shakespeare lived in the Liberty of the Clink, in Southwark, a short walk from the Globe Theatre.

The London I'd come to from the U.S.A. was a huge city, stretching for miles on both sides of the Thames. But this London seemed to be tiny, just the walled city that held the Tower, with villages dotted all around. And here in Southwark, just across the river, we were in a noisy seaport that was quite separate.

Because I was Nathan Field, the sheltered lad from St. Paul's School in the more law-abiding City of London, nobody would let me out in the streets of Southwark on my own. Mistress Fawcett wouldn't anyway, next morning, though I protested that I knew my way and that I had work to do. The play that day was to be *Henry V,* and when we weren't being princesses or waiting-women, we boys would be rushing on- or offstage as French or British soldiers, or both.

"Wait for Master Shakespeare," said Mistress Fawcett obstinately, putting her large self between me and the door. "He will leave for the playhouse in good time, he always does."

"But he's *writing*—"

I stopped, remembering. My father had been a writer. One year when Aunt Jen was into needlepoint, she'd made him a little rectangular cushion, bright green with black letters on it: MAN AT WORK. When his study door was shut and the cushion propped beside it, you didn't disturb him, not for anything. The only day when he hadn't thought to put the cushion outside his door was his last one.

I suddenly realized I was thinking about him, without panic or tears, in a way I hadn't done since he died.

But before I could wonder why, there was a great confused noise outside the front door: hoofbeats, and jingling harness, and men shouting. Mistress Fawcett frowned. Someone hammered at the door, and she frowned more darkly, and flung it open.

It was a serving man who had been doing the hammering, though he seemed to me as grandly dressed as a lord, with a gold crest embroidered on a red silk doublet. Out in the street behind him, in a straggle of gaping passersby, was a gleaming coach with four beautiful horses stamping and tossing their heads, and the same crest was painted on the coach doors.

The knocking man said loftily to Mistress Fawcett, "My Lord desires the presence of Master Shakespeare."

"Master Shakespeare is working," said Mistress Fawcett curtly. I got the feeling she'd come across my lord before and wasn't impressed.

The man stared at her. "Then he must stop!"

"Let be, Anthony," said a voice from the coach, and out of its shadowy inside stepped an amazing-looking young man: tall, handsome, swirling a brilliant yellow brocade cloak around his shoulders, wearing on his head a tall curly-feathered hat. He looked confident as a king, though there was something about his mouth that made me think of a spoiled little boy.

He glanced past Mistress Fawcett and me contemptuously, as if we weren't there, and automatically we moved to one side as he swept into the little hallway. "Will!" he called out, loud and imperious. "Will!"

Master Shakespeare must have heard the commotion already, because he was standing at the top of the stairs, with his doublet and shirt both unbuttoned and a quill pen still in his hand. He looked as if he had just come back from somewhere a long long way away, and left his head behind him.

"Go away," he said.

The young man paid no attention. "I must speak with thee!" he said, and he bounded up the stairs and swept Master Shakespeare back into his room. The door closed, and within a few seconds you could hear the indistinct blur of raised voices from inside.

Mistress Fawcett snorted indignantly, and slammed the front door in the face of the lordly serving man. She looked up the stairs, and then turned to me, with a small odd smile. "Nat," she said, "we are going to stay very quiet in thy room for a while."

Puzzled, I followed her through the kitchen into my tiny bedroom. She beckoned me toward the far wall, and she stood close to it, sideways, with her ear against the rough plaster. I tiptoed over and did the same—and coming down through the wall, perhaps through some air-filled gap between the laths, I could hear the voices from above. They were clear now. I glanced up at Mistress Fawcett; she put her finger to her lips.

"I will not!" said Master Shakespeare loudly, through the air and plaster.

"It would be so easy a thing!" said the nameless lord. His voice sounded exasperated. "Tell her an actor is sick, a major actor—so you cannot play the play."

"She would simply ask for another play, not requiring that actor."

"You said she particularly requested *A Midsummer Night's Dream.*"

"So she did, but also she is coming to see our new Globe Theatre, and sample the enjoyments of the common man. Of course, of course, the monarch does not go to a public theater—we take our plays to her at Court. When invited. But Gloriana is a monarch who does not always obey her own rules."

"Gloriana?" I looked at Mistress Fawcett. "Who's Gloriana?" I whispered.

"The Queen, of course!" she whispered, and frowned at me.

"And rash, and willful, and must be kept from dangers of her own making." The lord's voice softened, dropped, became cajoling. "Will, my dear—Sir Robert is much concerned over the perils of this escapade. If you would be in his good graces, you would do well to stop it happening."

"Is that a threat, my lord?" Shakespeare sounded icy.

"Of course not! But thy debt to Southampton and

thereby to Essex is well known, and that faction may be dangerous—"

"I have no debt!" Shakespeare shouted at him. There was a moment's pause, and then you could tell he was trying to control his voice, but it was still fierce and cross. "My lord, thou know'st I am not political. I am a tedious burgher from Stratford, a player, a maker of plays. I do not play games outside the theater—I have no desire to go the way of poor Kit Marlowe. And I will not take sides!"

There was the abrupt sound of his door opening, and Mistress Fawcett and I hastily jerked our heads away from the wall. She scuttled into the kitchen and busied herself with punching down a bowl of dough that sat rising on the table; I stayed in my little room, and listened to the blurred sound of footsteps on the stairs, voices at the door, and pretty soon the sounds of horses and carriage jingling and clattering away.

Shakespeare's voice came calling, clear and abrupt: "Nat! To the theater—now!"

He strode through the crowded, reeking, muddy streets of Southwark, so fast that I had to trot to keep up with him. "Factions!" he said irritably, half to himself. "Factions! A plague on both your houses!"

"*Romeo and Juliet,*" I said, smarty-pants, before I could stop myself.

Shakespeare glanced at me, distracted, and slowed his pace a little. "A sharp memory right enough, this boy Nathan. Hast played Juliet?"

"No," I said. I'd never fancied the lovey-dovey parts in his plays, even for the sake of being the lead.

"No," said Will Shakespeare, looking down at me as

he walked, reading my mind as usual. "Our Nat is not a romantic beauty. Th'art a sprite, an aerial sprite, born of the air. One day I shall write thee an airier Robin Good-fellow—unless thou leave me, or grow old."

He grinned at me, and for a moment I glowed all over and wanted to say: *I'll never leave you, I want to act with you forever.* Instead I said awkwardly, "Was he very important, that lord with the carriage?"

Shakespeare frowned. "He thinks himself so," he said, but he didn't tell me who the man had been. And the theater was looming ahead of us, with the white flag flying, and the usual bustle of people and horses and street vendors—and a large beruffed lady, her skirts trailing in the mud, shrieking after a running figure: "Cutpurse! Cutpurse! Stop, thief!"

But the scurrying thief escaped into the crowd, and Will Shakespeare and I into the door that led to the tiring-house, behind the stage.

In the boys' corner of the tiring-house, Roper was going through his lines with Thomas. He was to play the Boy in *Henry V*; it was a good part, this perky streetwise kid who hangs out with the roughneck soldiers Pistol and Bardolph and Nym, but is bright enough to deserve better. I'd met a few Boys back in twentieth-century America, and it wasn't hard to spot them on the streets of Elizabethan London. Maybe Roper was one himself—though he had a serious job as an apprentice, and if the company kept him on after his voice broke as a regular actor—a hired man—he'd have a good enough life.

I wondered whether that's what would happen to me, if I never managed to get back to my own time.

They were a funny sight, the two of them sitting there running lines: Roper in his streetboy costume, Thomas all painted and bewigged and gowned to play Alice, the French princess's attendant. They had reached the scene where Pistol has taken a French soldier prisoner in battle, but can't talk to him because he doesn't speak French. He's using the Boy, who's better educated, as interpreter.

Thomas read Roper his cue:

> *"Come hither, boy; ask me this slave in French*
> *What is his name."*

Roper said, pronouncing it exactly as it's written:

> *"Écoutez: comment êtes-vous appelé?"*

Thomas said, mildly, "You don't pronounce the *z* in *écoutez*. And the *e* isn't like English. It's not *ee-coo-tez*, it's *ay-coo-tay*. And the next part—"

Roper snorted in scorn. "Who do you think is going to know the difference?"

"Anyone who speaks French."

"Nobody in this audience will understand French, outside the Lords' Rooms."

Thomas rolled his eyes at me in mock horror, and I grinned at him. An hour or two earlier, he and Nick Tooley, who was playing the Princess Katharine, had been onstage rehearsing a scene Master Shakespeare had written entirely in French. Probably Roper knew only his own scenes.

Thomas said to me, "*Parlez-vous français,* Nat?"

"*Bien sûr,*" I said, because I did know some French—not much, but a year's worth. "*Je parle français. Un peu.*"

Roper glared at me. "Who asked you?"

"Well, Thomas did, actually. In French."

"Trust the little lass from St. Paul's to have some girl-ish talent to brag about," said Roper nastily. "I don't want a French lesson, Thomas, I just want to run my lines."

"Very well," Thomas said amiably, and Roper went on spouting his impossible English French. I listened, re-membering the lines from the time I'd played the Boy in Washington, D.C., when I hadn't understood any French words either. I'd had a terrible time learning the right way to say them, which is I suppose why they stuck. Roper clearly hadn't had a terrible time—he'd barely tried.

By the time the trumpeter climbed up above the stage to blow the fanfare that began the play, we boys were all dressed up as pages and attendants for a court scene, and the men in gorgeous robes: Master Burbage as King Henry, Henry Condell as the Archbishop of Canterbury, very grand. As usual, there were constant nervous visits to the "plot," the list of entrances and exits that hung near the stage in the tiring-house, and whenever Master Burbage came offstage he made a beeline for the book-keeper, a small bespectacled man who sat beside a window—out of the traffic but handy to the stage—with the play's text on his lap.

"What's next, after the Boar's Head, what's next?"

"Be calm, Dick. The traitors' scene—'*Now sits the wind fair, and we will aboard. . . .*'"

Burbage went away muttering: "*Now sits the wind*

fair. . . ." and the tireman seized him, to change his robe.

Everyone always had trouble remembering lines, under the pressure of five different plays to perform every week, and there was a fair bit of improvising. "Thribbling," they called it; isn't that a great word? But when the play was by Will Shakespeare, actors tried not to thribble, because Master Shakespeare was not pleased when people put in words that were not his own. Thomas said this had been the main reason for Shakespeare's row with Will Kempe, who was inclined to make winking asides to the audience in the hope of getting an extra laugh.

Henry V went wonderfully well. Burbage was a terrific Henry, and the groundlings loved him; they cheered when he swashbuckled, and stood still as mice when he had a quiet moving speech, like the one that begins *"Upon the King. . . ."* They were hugely patriotic; they hissed the French so fiercely that it was quite frightening to come onstage as a French soldier and see all those hostile faces scowling and shouting at you. They also cheered something that surprised me—but before that there was a bit of drama that surprised me even more.

Roper had come offstage after a scene in Act Three that had included his biggest speech; he'd done it really well, and got a lot of laughs from the groundlings. I wanted to tell him it was good, because we were all actors, even though he was such a pain—but he was full of himself, and kicked at me when he found me in his way, though not with enough concentration to hit me. After that I forgot about him, because the rest of us had to mill about onstage as French soldiers—but once we were back, there he was again, stirring things up even though Master Burbage was onstage doing Henry's best big speech.

"We few, we happy few, we band of brothers. . . ."

I was standing in the tiring-house trying to listen, when Roper came slipping past me, snatched an apple from the tireman's table, and started to chomp on it. Eating backstage was strictly forbidden while a performance was going on, and the man reached out to grab him, hissing a warning. Roper took a bigger bite, dancing out of his way, chewing, mouthing some cocky jeer as he moved—and then he choked.

He stopped absolutely still, clutching his throat; after one awful first croak he didn't make a sound. A piece of apple must have gone right into his windpipe. Onstage, a cheer went up as Burbage finished his speech, and John Heminges, all in armor as Lord Salisbury, rushed onstage through an entry door. Augustine Phillips as the French herald Mountjoy waited for his cue at the opposite side. Neither of them noticed the bigger drama going on backstage as everyone not in the scene hurried to crowd around Roper, banging him on the back, desperately trying to save him. He stood there terrified, suffocating, his face a dusky red, his eyes popping; in all the turmoil he could do nothing but flap his hands in a speechless plea for help.

I didn't *think*, really; I just knew what they ought to be doing, because Aunt Jen had taught me, the year before, when she was taking some lifesaving course at the Red Cross. I ran over to Roper and shoved Nick aside, spilling the water he was trying to get Roper to drink.

"Look out!" I said, and I stood behind Roper, put my arms around him, made a fist with one hand between his ribs and his belly button, put my other hand over it, and jerked in and upward, hard. So the air was pushed up out of Roper's lungs, up through his windpipe, and the piece of apple popped out. It fell out of his mouth and he hung there over my arm, making awful noises, great croaking gasps for air. But he was breathing.

The voices from the stage went echoing on around us, but everyone backstage was staring at me. I looked at them, and felt uneasy; they looked almost as scared as they had when he was choking.

Nick said, amazed, "What did you do?"

I guess I babbled, because I was nervous. I said, "It's called the Heimlich maneuver, some guy called Heimlich invented it—" And they went on staring, and I realized too late that I was sounding completely like a modern kid, because in Elizabethan England they didn't use the word *guy* or probably the word *maneuver* either, and how could they know who Mr. Heimlich was, when he wasn't going to be born for hundreds of years yet?

I said lamely, "My aunt showed me how."

Then Roper rescued me. He threw up on the floor.

And suddenly the book-keeper was there, very agitated, with the actors playing Pistol and the French soldier, and he was hissing at us to be ready to run onstage fighting, for the battle scene out of which Pistol would seize the Frenchman prisoner.

Pistol looked in horror at Roper's white face. "What ails the boy! Our cue is next! We need him!"

I didn't think this time either, I just jumped in again—

and this time my brain nearly died of shock when it heard what I said.

"I can do it," I said. "I know the scene."

Theater people can move very fast sometimes. In that theater particularly, I guess they were used to people being able to jump into other people's parts in an emergency. Before you could blink, the book-keeper whipped off the French soldier's surcoat I was wearing, and the tireman pulled Roper's jerkin off his back and onto mine. Thomas grabbed up Roper's pages from somewhere and thrust them under my nose, for a quick frantic reminding look, and then fireworks were being set off onstage in a sequence of huge bangs, and clouds of smoke from a crude smoke machine being puffed out from a backstage bellows, for the battle effects, and Pistol grabbed my arm. And we were on.

The first few lines of that scene belong just to Pistol and the French soldier, fortunately. It gave me a chance to get my bearings, before the dreaded cue.

> "*Come hither, boy; ask me this slave in French*
> *What is his name.*"

I almost shouted my line, I was so nervous:

> "*Écoutez: comment êtes-vous appelé?*"

I forget the actor's name, but he sounded marvelously French. "*Monsieur le Fer,*" he said.

The next line was easy to remember. I said to Pistol:

> "*He says his name is Master Fer.*"

Pistol rolled his drunken eyes. *"Master Fer! I'll fer him, and firk him, and ferret him—discuss the same in French unto him."*

There was a ripple of laughter from the audience, and a drunken voice from the yard shouted, "Ferret him! Ferret him!" But my next line came into my head too.

"I do not know the French for fer, and ferret, and firk."

That got a real laugh, probably helped by the fact my voice went up into a squeak because I was so scared—and then suddenly I was all right, I was the Boy, I was acting, and we went sailing through the scene, loudmouthed Pistol and the terrified French prisoner and me. I picked up the cues, I remembered the French speeches—there were only two really—and the audience carried us along. The other two were really good actors, caricature-funny; the groundlings loved them.

My only bad moment was my last speech, the Boy alone onstage after the other two have gone off; I did an awful lot of thribbling. But I was helped by the fact that I'd come way downstage, so that I was right on top of the groundlings: I fixed my eyes on one man near the front, with a round red face and two front teeth missing, and said everything right to him. It was a perfect eye contact; he was gaping at me, fascinated. And I did remember to say the last line, telling that the English camp was guarded only by boys—and that was the most important, because what happens then is that the French invade the camp and murder all the boys, and that makes King Henry truly furious.

So it all went okay, and I slipped offstage as the French

soldiers came running on the other side. I'm not sure the audience ever knew or cared that they'd been watching a different Boy from the last one they'd seen. A boy was a boy; what they cared about was the story.

In the tiring-house I ran straight into Roper, and he threw his arms around me. He smelled terrible, because of having thrown up. I guess he knew that, since he let me go almost at once, but he stood there looking at me very seriously. He said, "I thought I was dead. Tha saved my life."

"And me only a little lass," I said.

Roper looked down at his feet. He said, rather muffled, "Tha saved me a beating too. Missing that cue—missing that scene—Master Burbage would have—"

"Cut off thine ears," I said. "One by one, very slowly, inch by inch." I grinned at him, which took some effort because my doing the Heimlich business had nothing to do with him. As far as I was concerned he was the same mean little monster he'd been before. He didn't grin back; he went on giving me this same earnest look. I think Roper was feeling an emotion he'd never had to cope with before: guilt.

"I am in thy debt, Nathan Field," he said stiffly. "I shall not forget."

He patted me on the shoulder and I gave a sort of awkward shrug. I was wishing I knew the Elizabethan way to say, "Okay—just stop bugging me from now on."

Will Shakespeare came sweeping past us toward the stage, pulling on the robe he wore as Chorus, ignoring an anxious tireman running after him with his hat. He caught sight of me, and stopped suddenly, and the tireman bumped into him, frantically holding out the hat so it wouldn't get squashed. From the stage we heard a great cheer; Master

Burbage had reached the end of the scene in which King Henry hears that his little army of Brits have managed to kill ten thousand Frenchmen in battle while losing only twenty-nine men themselves. (Ten thousand? Are you kidding me?)

Shakespeare paused for a moment, gazing at me, but he had no chance to say anything, because his cue had come: the tireman plunked his hat on his head, straightened it, and pushed him around to face the stage. And as Master Burbage came stalking backstage through the door stage right, out went Will Shakespeare stage left, to face the world, our world, the audience.

> *"Vouchsafe to those that have not read the story*
> *That I may prompt them. . . ."*

I stood behind the stage hangings, listening. He had a wonderful voice, clear and warm and sort of mid-brown. I was as happy that moment as I think I'll ever be: standing there listening to him, knowing I was part—and a useful part, just now—of his company, safe in the small family world of the theater. I wanted it never to end.

Shakespeare went on with that speech that tells the audience how King Henry is now coming back in triumph to London from France, and I was half hearing it, half just enjoying the sound of his voice, when a few particular words came, interrupting my vague head because suddenly they didn't make sense.

> *"Were now the General of our gracious Empress—*
> *As in good time he may—from Ireland coming,*
> *Bringing rebellion broached upon his sword,*

> *How many would the peaceful city quit*
> *To welcome him!"*

Empress? Ireland? I didn't understand. I'd never noticed that part before. And then there was a huge cheer from the audience at the word *welcome,* so that Master Shakespeare had to wait for them to quiet down before he could go on.

> *"Much more, and much more cause*
> *Did they this Harry. . . ."*

Close to me, Tom the book-keeper was sitting with his script, listening, looking sour. I said in his ear, "What are they shouting about?"

"Essex, of course," he said. "Where hast'a been, boy? Pretty Robin, Earl of Essex, who is in Ireland about the Queen's business putting down rebellion. And let's hope, not starting one of his own." But he dropped his voice on this last bit, and his eyes flickered cautiously to and fro.

I remembered Will Shakespeare protesting that morning to the nameless lord that he was not political, and wondered why, in that case, he had dropped such an obvious compliment to the Earl of Essex into his *Henry V.*

It didn't seem to bother Roper, who was clapping along with the audience, his face bright and intent. Behind him in the shadowy tiring-house I saw Master Burbage, listening too, caught into stillness after his bustling exit from the stage. He was King Henry, confident and magnificent in his gleaming armor, but suddenly his face was quite different. He was shaking his head, uneasy. He looked frightened.

ELEVEN

I began to be frightened too, that evening, for the first time—even through the delight I had from being with Will Shakespeare, being one of the Chamberlain's Men. Partly I was afraid of this business about the Earl of Essex, whatever it was. Shakespeare had some connection with him, the nameless lord had called him dangerous, Master Burbage was clearly nervous—and worst of all, though I could remember very little about Arby's potted history of Elizabethan England, I did remember that Queen Elizabeth had had Essex's head chopped off. So that Essex was about to end up, sooner or later, among those terrible pecked-at skulls stuck up over London Bridge.

Why did that happen, and when? I was afloat in Time, I didn't know where I was.

But I did know one other thing that worried me. In less than twenty-four hours' time, we would perform *A Midsummer Night's Dream* in front of the Queen, and after that the Chamberlain's Men would have no more need for Nathan Field, and he would be sent back to St. Paul's School, where he came from. What would become of me then? I should lose Will Shakespeare—and be faced with the friends and family of the real Nathan, who would instantly know that whoever I was, I was certainly not

Nathan Field. If I felt I had very little place in my own world anymore, I was going to have even less in this one. It was terrifying, like facing a drop over a huge cliff.

In fact it was so terrifying that I pushed it out of my head, and tried to concentrate on the shadowy Earl of Essex instead.

After *Henry V* and a break, we rehearsed *A Midsummer Night's Dream* until dark, though without Bottom the Weaver, because Master Burbage was exhausted. He took a nap on a mattress at the back of the tiring-house, oblivious of us. I loved doing my scenes with Will Shakespeare—and I loved our costumes, which the tireman produced for a fitting. They were wildly fantastical; Shakespeare had shimmering robes over a bare chest and full, shot-silk pants, with a weird headdress and antennae on his head.

I was to wear gleaming green tights, like the skin of some exotic snake, and nothing else but a lot of body paint. The tireman told me that the tights had cost the equivalent of six months of his wages, so that he would personally destroy me if I tore them. He showed me a drawing of the design for the makeup on the rest of me. "Master Burbage will paint you," he said, "but not till the day. It will take almost an hour."

Shakespeare said to me, as we were waiting for an entrance, "I hear thou leapt into the breach this afternoon."

"It was good luck," I said. I was going to tell him I'd played the Boy before, but I suddenly remembered that it was a new play. "Uh—I'd been listening to Roper rehearse, and I have a memory like a sponge. So I remembered his lines."

It sounded improbable, but he seemed to believe it.

"And what ailed our friend Roper?" he said.

"He was ill," I said evasively. "Something he ate."

Will Shakespeare looked down at me with an odd smile. "My small magician," he said. And then it was our cue, and we went through the door to the stage.

The other boys were more interested in Roper's choking and its cure than in my having done his scene. They made me uneasy: they were looking at me warily, as if I'd grown another head. Harry said, "What didst tha *do* to him?"

"If someone chokes, you hold him from behind and push hard into his belly, so the air pushes up out of his lungs and blows out whatever he's choking on. That's all."

"Who taught thee how?"

"My aunt. I told you."

Harry and fair-haired Nick Tooley looked at each other like conspirators. Nick said, "Is she a wise woman?"

"Well, I suppose so," I said. It wasn't quite how I would have described Aunt Jen, who is a perky little person with a grey ponytail.

"Ah," said Nick, and nodded his head. He and Harry looked at each other again, and then at me, with what I felt was a mixture of respect and fear. It was creepy.

After rehearsal Will Shakespeare went with five other actors to a tavern not far from the Globe, to eat supper and drink and talk. He took me with him, which was great by me. Harry came too, because Master Burbage didn't want to pay for two river crossings home to Shoreditch in one night. The tavern was noisy and smoky, full of shouting red-faced men, and bustling girls trying to carry trays of mugs and avoid having their bottoms pinched; Master

Burbage led the way right through the main room to a quieter one at the back. We sat at a battered, heavy wooden table and ate bowls of a really good kind of stew, spicy, with onions in it, and hunks of new bread, and afterward Harry and I drank cider and tried not to fall asleep.

The actors fell into separate serious conversations—Master Burbage particularly earnest with Will Shakespeare, away in a corner, the two of them alone together. Pretty soon Harry and I were slumped against the wall near the glowing wood fire, which was comforting because the nights were decidedly cool even though it was August. At least, it was August in the world I had come from, so I assumed it was the same here. I never saw a calendar, and I never thought to ask. This London had all its bells ringing to tell you what time of day or night it was, but those were the only landmarks of Time to be seen or heard.

I said, "Harry, is it something special, to be a wise woman?"

Harry was drooping over his mug. He yawned. "A wise woman is a witch, of course."

I felt suddenly cold. Harry blinked himself awake, and caught sight of my face. "What ails thee?"

"Nick Tooley said—about my Aunt Jen—"

Harry laughed. "Bless thee—anyone would be glad of a white witch in the family, to heal the sick and save life. Even Roper's life."

"But—people burned witches—"

"Not unless they do harm." He hoisted himself upright, back against the wall. "Th'art an odd one, Nat

Field—th'art such an innocent. Like a baby. Tha knowst so much, and then sometimes tha knows nothing."

"I've led a quiet life," I said. I took a breath. "Tell me about the Earl of Essex."

Harry took a swig of cider, and wiped his mouth on his sleeve. "Tell what?" he said cautiously.

"Anything."

He shrugged. "Well, he is a fine lord, and handsome. We played at his great house, my first year as apprentice, and the Queen was there. She laughed with him a lot, and they whispered together. He was her favorite then. He is Earl Marshal of England, and they still cheer him in the streets."

I said, "They cheered the lines about him in the play today."

"Aye. But he angered the Queen somehow, he angers Robert Cecil who leads her Privy Council. Now he is in Ireland, with Will Shakespeare's patron Southampton, sent to stop the Irish from joining with our enemies in Spain. But my father says he is all ambition, he is dangerous."

There was that word again. "What sort of dangerous?"

Harry looked around nervously, though there was nobody in the room except our masters, drinking ale and spouting solemn words at one another. "The Queen is growing old, and has not said who will succeed her. London is full of spies—Spain longs to take England—" He stopped, and looked at me helplessly. "Dost not know *any* of this, Nat?"

I hung my head and tried to look dim-witted. "There is no chance to hear street talk at St. Paul's—we are shut up like little nuns."

"Nobody trusts anybody, that is the sum of it. They talk of plots, of assassinations—the Queen's doctor was hanged and quartered two years ago, because Essex said he'd tried to poison her." Harry glanced across at Master Burbage, still deep in talk with Will Shakespeare. "And those who know she is coming to our theater are frightened of it, they think people might do her harm. Master Burbage would stop her coming if he could."

"He's afraid of the *people*? The audience?"

"You heard how they cheered my Lord of Essex, who is on the outs with her."

I looked at Richard Burbage, leaning forward anxiously to Will Shakespeare, tapping one long finger on the table to make a point. I saw Shakespeare shake his head vigorously; then he pushed back his chair with a screeching, scraping noise, and stood up. He called to me, pulling on his cloak.

"Nat? Come away, boy. Time to go home."

So the party broke up, and everyone went off into the dark night to their respective homes. Master Shakespeare and I trudged in silence through the streets of Southwark to his lodging, in the company of a hired linkman: a kind of bodyguard, who carried a burning torch that gave off some light and a lot of bitter-smelling smoke, and had a heavy stick in his other hand to fight off anyone who tried to rob us. I don't know why they were called linkmen, but they were nearly always big battered-looking fellows with large muscles and a few missing teeth, and the muscles were reassuring. Since there were no policemen in Elizabethan London, and no streetlights, there was no shortage of robbers and other villains. It was wise not to go out alone at night, not without a dagger or a sword or a linkman, or all three.

A fine drizzle began to fall, and I was damp and dismal by the time we reached the lodging. Mistress Fawcett had left two candles on the chest just inside the front door, with flint and steel; Shakespeare lit them. They burned with a smoky, flickering flame, and the house was full of dark dancing shadows. I only had to live in an Elizabethan house for one night to long for flashlights, and lightbulbs, and a switch to turn darkness into light.

I took my candle, mournfully. All my worries were thronging round my head, and now the distant Earl of Essex was the least of them; I could think of nothing but my despair at the prospect of having to leave Will Shakespeare.

I said, rather wobbly, and quietly so as not to wake Mistress Fawcett, "Master Shakespeare?"

He was about to climb the stair to his room. He looked tired, his eyes shadowed. "What is it?"

"When the play is over—instead of going back to St. Paul's—could I—would you take me as your apprentice?"

Shakespeare laughed abruptly, in surprise; but he held up his candle and saw my face, and stopped laughing. "Nat, my dear—th'art enrolled at St. Paul's, th'art one of Richard Mulcaster's prize actors, I am told. He would never let thee go."

I couldn't explain to him, I couldn't tell him Richard Mulcaster would take one look at me and demand the real Nathan Field. Maybe I would even be accused of having murdered him, in this dangerous world where Roper had seen throats cut.

I said miserably, "I shall be so lonely."

Shakespeare put his hand on my shoulder. He was thinking of me as the orphan boy, I knew; thinking my head was haunted only by the death of my father—as it had been, too, until now. Perhaps he was thinking of his own boy Hamnet as well.

"Go—get into thy nightshirt," he said. "And I will bring thee something."

The little room behind the kitchen was warmer than the hallway had been, but still chilly. I scrambled out of my damp clothes and into my thick linen nightshirt, draped the clothes over a chair, and huddled down under the blankets. The candle by my bed sent a thin stream of black smoke quivering up to the ceiling, and the shadows swung and flickered on the wall. Then new shadows danced over them, and Will Shakespeare came into the room. He was carrying his own candle in one hand, and a sheet of paper in the other.

He went down on one knee beside the bed, probably feeling the little bedstead would collapse under him if he sat on it, and he showed me the paper. "This is a sonnet I copied for thee after we talked the other day," he said. "It is about love, and loving. I wrote it for a woman, but it could just as well be for thee and thy father. I give it you to remind you that love does not vanish with death."

I looked at the page; it was covered in the cramped Elizabethan handwriting that I could never understand.

I said, "Will you read it to me?"

Shakespeare looked a little taken aback, but not displeased. He was an actor, after all. He tilted the page so that the candlelight shone on it, and very quietly and simply, he read me the poem.

"Let me not to the marriage of true minds
Admit impediments. Love is not love
Which alters when it alteration finds
Or bends with the remover to remove.
O, no! It is an ever-fixed mark
That looks on tempests and is never shaken;
It is the star to every wand'ring bark
Whose worth's unknown, although his height be taken.
Love's not Time's fool, though rosy lips and cheeks
Within his bending sickle's compass come;
Love alters not with his brief hours and weeks,
But bears it out, even to the edge of doom.
If this be error, and upon me prov'd,
I never writ, nor no man ever lov'd."

Before I could say anything, he held out the page to me, and stood up. "I have no picture of what may become of us after we are dead, Nat," he said. "But I do know thy father's love for thee did not die with him, nor thine for him. Nor mine for my Hamnet—or for this lady. Love is love. An ever-fixed mark. Remember that, and try to be comforted."

He said "fixed" as if it had two syllables. I remember that.

I took the stiff, curling paper, and put it carefully smooth under my pillow. "Thank you very, very much," I said.

"Sleep well, sprite," Shakespeare said. He bent down and kissed me on the forehead. Then he blew out my candle, and went out, carrying his own. The shadows flickered away with him, and left the room dark.

TWELVE

Mrs. Fisher stands at the Information desk of Guy's Hospital, on the Southwark bank of the River Thames. She's waiting for someone to become free to speak to her; this is a huge and very busy hospital. Beside her stands a smallish woman in the trademark raincoat of the American tourist visiting England; her face looks younger than her grey hair. She is Jennifer Field, who has flown from Greenville, South Carolina, to London, alarmed by the astounding news that her nephew Nat is in the hospital suffering from bubonic plague. She looks around her at the bustling, echoing lobby of the hospital, feeling lost.

"I don't know which ward," Mrs. Fisher is saying now to a friendly face behind the desk. "They've had him isolated, on the top floor. It's Nathan Field, his doctor is Dr. Ravi Singh."

The friendly person taps at her computer keyboard, and inspects the screen. "I'm afraid you can't see him. Not yet."

"But this is the right time for visiting hours, isn't it?"

"I'm awfully sorry, but it says 'Absolutely No Visitors' against his name."

"This lady is his aunt, she's flown all the way from America to see him."

"Tell you what," says the friendly person, "I'll let you talk to the duty nurse."

She reaches for the telephone, and soon Jennifer Field is explaining herself to the soothing voice of Nurse Stevens.

"Tomorrow," says Nurse Stevens. "Or maybe the day after. Hasn't Dr. Singh reached you yet? You'll see your nephew, you might even be taking him out. He's much better, we took him off his IV this morning."

"But can't I just see him for a moment now? He'd love to see someone from home. This is crazy—what harm could it possibly do?"

Nurse Stevens is inclined to agree, but Dr. Singh is strict, and orders are orders. "I'm sorry, really I am, but Dr. Singh wants to be careful, it being such a rare disease. Don't worry, Miss Field—Nathan's going to be fine."

Jennifer Field says rebelliously, "This is all nonsense. I'm going to call Dr. Singh."

"Please do," Nurse Stevens says.

"Well—thank you. It's not your fault, I guess. Tell Nat— tell him Aunt Jen is here, and sends him a big hug."

"Indeed I will," says Nurse Stevens. "Good-bye." And she puts down the phone, up in the high ward, and wonders how best to communicate this message to the strange boy with the heavy accent that is not quite American and not quite West Country English. He is no longer really ill, thanks to the antibiotics, but seems wholly disoriented, with no idea of where he is or what has been happening to him.

And what on earth, she wonders, can his background be like? He seems never to have seen a thermometer before, or a washbasin, or even a toilet. He fought like a tiger the first time she tried to put a blood pressure cuff around his arm, and when he had his first glimpse out the window of this fifteenth-floor room, he screamed. As for his personal habits. . . . He picks up food with his fingers, or on the point of his knife, and everything goes downhill from there on. Nurse Stevens plans to get him into a bath today, and to wash his long hair. She expects to become very wet in the process.

She opens the door to Nathan Field's room, and sees his wide-eyed unhappy face turn toward her, on the pillow.

"I want to go home," he says. "Prithee, ask thy master to let me go home."

THIRTEEN

We were up with the sun the morning of the performance. The sky was a hazy blue, and the birds were shouting. I was so nervous I didn't want any breakfast, but Mistress Fawcett made me sit down and eat a bowl of bread and milk. It sounds awful—cubes of bread soaked in warm milk, sweetened—but it was comforting, and the idea of it must have survived the centuries, because Aunt Jen used to give me the same thing when I was sick. Once when I had the chicken pox I wouldn't eat anything else for three days.

Will Shakespeare was so nervous he wouldn't eat anything at all. He changed his doublet three times in half an hour, and looked no better in the third than he had in the first. Unlike Master Burbage, he had very little of the peacock in him, and all his clothes were serviceable rather than showy. Even his one gold earring was very small. Mistress Fawcett had told me that within the past year he'd bought a big house in Stratford, his home in Warwickshire, and that he would be paying for it for some time yet.

When he was back in the brown doublet and white shirt that he had started with, we walked to the theater, over the square cobbles of the street, which were hard and lumpy through the thin leather soles of Elizabethan shoes. It had rained during the night, and the roofs and roads were still gleaming and new-washed; the crows were hopping and quarreling over garbage, here and there, but the smells weren't so bad as usual.

Wagons were creaking through the streets, loaded with sacks and baskets of fruit and vegetables from the country, for early delivery; the horses' hooves clopped over the cobbles, echoing to and fro. You had to dodge them, but you could walk without the constant shock of hands tugging at you, because the beggars weren't about yet: the dirty barefoot children; the old soldiers missing an arm or a leg or an eye, or all three; the hollow-eyed, stringy-haired women with whimpering babies in their skinny arms. Ahead of us, over the rippling green tree-tops, the flag was already flying from the roof of the Globe, announcing that a play would be given there today. Not many people knew quite how special this perfor-mance would be.

Will Shakespeare was striding along, silent. I had to hurry to keep up.

I said, tentatively, trotting at his side, "Do we know if . . . Do we know who will be there?"

"If there are soldiers, that will tell thee," he said. And that was all he said, until we reached the Globe.

In the theater, even though it was so early, Richard Burbage was onstage with the other "mechanicals," re-hearsing their Pyramus and Thisbe play. They were very funny, especially round-faced Henry Condell as Moon-shine. While I was watching, I completely forgot to won-der about the Queen. I stood in the tiring-house, peeking at them from the corner where the book-keeper would sit, trying not to snort with laughter—though it's a rare actor who objects to hearing a laugh, unless of course he's trying to make people cry.

There was a sort of scuffling behind me, and I glanced around. Two of the extra men, hired by the day to help fetch and carry, were dragging in a rolled stage hanging, a long, unwieldy cylinder of painted canvas. I knew them both by sight; they'd been in the theater for most of the week. They caught sight of me, and the first one stopped in his tracks and stood stone-still, so that the second tripped over the canvas and yelped crossly at him. The other began to move again—but before that, just for a moment, he raised one hand at me with the first and fourth fingers pointing, and the others clenched into the palm by the thumb. It was a swift little gesture, but unmistakable. Then they laid the stage hanging at the back of the room, and were gone.

But I'd seen that gesture before, four hundred years later, in a play, and so I knew what it meant. It was very old, and I think it came from Europe. It was a sign to ward off the evil eye.

Clearly at least one person in this company thought I might be a witch.

Later in the morning, the soldiers came. They weren't very obtrusive, and they weren't your basic ordinary foot soldiers; they were quiet, sharp-eyed men, with gleaming armor under their expensive cloaks, and they went through every smallest closet and cranny of the Globe

Theatre. I don't know what they were looking for; I don't know whether people made bombs in those days, though even if they did, I'm sure they couldn't have set them off by detonator, or remote control. At any rate the soldiers didn't seem to find anything. We kept running into them around corners, but they paid us no attention; they just went about their business and so did we, and after about an hour we started taking them for granted as a necessary nuisance.

By now everyone in the company knew that Her Majesty the Queen might be sitting up in one of the gallery rooms at this performance, behind a curtain—and everyone in the company, even those who had played several times at Court, was shaking with nervousness. They had lots of reasons, of course, but I think a very large one was the fact that they all loved their new Globe Theatre, and were proud of it—and they wanted to do it credit. It was almost as if they wanted their theater to be proud of *them*.

Around noon, Richard Burbage had me pull off my shirt, and stood me in front of him in the corner of the tiring-house where he kept his paints. Then he began putting on my body makeup for Puck. Although he was an actor—which was no surprise, since his father had been England's first real theater manager—he was also a really good painter, and whenever one of the Lord Chamberlain's Men needed a special makeup, he would beg Burbage to do it. I didn't have to beg; he was determined to turn me into an unearthly, magical, and faintly scary spirit. After about fifteen minutes my face, neck, arms, and upper body were all a spooky green, and he was about to start on the elaborate details.

"Stand still, boy!" He was starting a long straight line from neck to wrist, all the way down my arm. It was the stem from which many intertwining leaves would grow and curl.

"I'm sorry. It tickles."

"I'll tickle thee with my boot if tha moves again. Joseph, where are his hose?"

"Safe and out of harm's way until th'art done," said the tireman cautiously. He was always very nervous of Master Burbage's wet paint when valuable costumes were nearby.

"Well, fetch them out, fool! I have to match the color. Nobody will mar them—thou may'st hold them in thy hand all the while." Burbage paused, and gave the tireman the eye-crinkling smile that always made people forgive him for yelling at them. It reminded me of Arby. "And th'art a good fellow for guarding company property so well."

The tireman snorted, but mildly, and went to get my tights. Will Shakespeare came from behind me, pulled up a stool and sat down to watch Burbage paint. Gladness at seeing him sent a sudden warmth into my throat and my chest; a wonderful feeling, but oddly like pain.

The brush flickered, and leaves sprouted swiftly around my wrist, and up my forearm. "Thy turn next, Will," Burbage said. "How does our house?"

"There is a line down the street fifty yards long."

"Even without them knowing. It is a good draw, thy *Dream*."

"And will be very beautiful, this time," Shakespeare said.

Burbage looked pleased, and drew a tendril around

my right ear, with his tongue curled carefully over his upper lip. I knew he had taken great care with new designs for this production, and spent lavishly on some new costumes, which most of us had not yet seen.

From outside, the noise of the crowd began to drift in: muffled shouts and laughter, as tumblers, jugglers and fire-eaters struggled for the attention of the waiting audience in the street. You couldn't buy tickets in advance at theaters then; you had to wait in line, pay your penny admission at the door to the "gatherer," and run to get a good place in the yard. Or, alternatively, you went to the staircase, paid another penny to another gatherer, and scurried up narrow stairs and along rows of narrow benches to get a good place in one of the galleries. There you would have a good view of the play from a hard wooden bench, which would be made slightly more comfortable by a pillow if you'd brought one with you, or paid yet another penny to rent one.

It all sounds cheap, I guess, a penny here, a penny there, but it wasn't cheap then—I'd listened to Mistress Fawcett complaining about prices and wages. For a penny you could buy a pound of cheese, or half a pound of butter; six pints of beer, or a big two-pound loaf of bread. But a workman like a carpenter or a mason only earned about thirty pence a week—so I guess groundlings didn't go to the theater too often. Mind you, that didn't stop them from buying munchies from the sellers who wandered about the theater with baskets and trays. Just the way you might buy popcorn or soda at the movies, they'd buy apples, or bags of nuts, bottles of beer or ginger ale. Master Shakespeare once said that he knew he'd written a really good scene if it caught the groundlings' attention long enough to stop them cracking nuts.

"Turn round, Nat," said Master Burbage, and he started painting long strands of flowering vines across my back. At least, that's what they told me later; all I could feel was the small traveling chill of the brush and the wet paint.

"Much more of this, and the boy's fingertips will burst into bloom," Will Shakespeare said.

"That is my aim," said Burbage. "I plan for clusters of dog rose. Go away for ten minutes, Will, go study thy lines. Write the stage-keepers some birdsong."

Shakespeare laughed, but he did cast an anxious eye about for the stage-keepers. These were the extra men, the dailies, like the two I'd seen carrying canvas; whenever there were no actors to spare, they had to move props, carry furniture, help to create special effects. They would be busy backstage making the forest magical in *A Midsummer Night's Dream*: blowing a little pipe into a bowl of water to make the sounds of birdsong; burning rope in a metal pot, to make smoke that could be puffed with a bellows across the stage, for romantic mist or bewildering fog. The groundlings were very fond of special effects. They particularly liked disasters, and explosions. They'd have loved video games.

The tiring-house was getting more crowded now, as the day wore on toward afternoon. All the boys but me were playing women in this play, and extra tiremen were on duty, carrying in the long elaborate dresses from back rooms, painting faces with the white cheeks and black-rimmed eyes that were standard for a stage female. The few doors and windows stood wide open, to let in air; it was a warm day, and the enclosed space was growing hot and stuffy. Flies buzzed everywhere, slow and sleepy.

Out in the theater it was hot too; the sun stood high in the sky, beating down through the open center of the roof. For a while it would blaze into the faces of half the audience, and the ladies who had brought fans would have to choose whether to fan themselves, or to hold up the fan as an eyeshade against the bright light. The drink sellers would do a roaring trade.

Richard Burbage finished his painting and handed me into the care of the tireman, Joseph, to keep me from smudging his beautiful paint before it dried. Then it was Will Shakespeare's turn to pull off his shirt and stand still to be made magical.

Joseph, a small brown man with a completely bald head, drew me into a corner free of traffic and poured me into my snakey green tights. He showed me myself in a rather dim, distorted mirror, and even that blurry reflection was phenomenal: I saw a glimmering green woodland sprite, the perfect image for the lines I would speak. The ears were pointed, the eyebrows slanted up, the eyes were big and dark like the eyes of a fawn. I wasn't me anymore, nor even Nathan Field. I was Puck. Shakespeare's Puck.

"Now up aloft with thee, out of the way, until we begin," Joseph said. He pushed me toward the ladder that led to the "heavens," the room behind the stage gallery where the musicians would sit, and I climbed up.

Out in the theater the noise level began to rise, as the audience came in. Peeking through the door that led to the gallery, I could see the benches and yard filling with sturdy shopkeepers and craftsmen and their smiling beribboned wives, apprentices, students and even a few children. The spaces filled up, all three thousand of them, so far as I could tell, and the noise of all their different voices grew and grew.

I stood gazing, with the noise thrumming through my head, and didn't hear Will Shakespeare come up the stairs behind me.

"Listen to it," he said in my ear, his hands resting lightly on my painted shoulders. "All those voices which become one—the voice of that single great animal, the audience. The Leviathan. A very large and frightening animal—*which we shall tame.*"

I glanced up over my shoulder at his face. His eyes were gleaming, out of the dark makeup that was just as fantastic and unearthly as my own, and he was smiling. This was his world, this was what he did and who he was, and I knew exactly how he was feeling, because the same was true for me. I knew too that I didn't need to say so. I smiled back at him.

Suddenly there was a sharper eruption of noise, out in the audience, and I peeked through the part-open door again. I saw a flurry of movement down in the yard, and heard voices raised: "Thief! Stop, thief!" A man was diving through the crowd, weaving, dodging, but too many hands reached out for him, and soon he was struggling in the arms of two particularly large groundlings. I saw one of them wrench a leather purse away from him. He was a small, thin man, not much more than a boy.

"Cutpurse," said Shakespeare. He sighed, and turned away.

People who worked hard for their pence had no sympathy for cutpurses, the Elizabethan equivalent of pickpockets, who carried a sharp little knife to cut through the leather thong that attached a money pouch to a belt. A quick jostle in the crowd, and a purse was gone, and with it half a week's earnings, or more.

The cutpurse was being hustled, kicking and wriggling, toward the stage. One of his captors had gotten some rope from somewhere, perhaps from one of the gatherers who were used to this kind of thing, and he and some others hauled the boy up onto the stage and tied him to one of the big front stage pillars. There he stood, wretched and exposed, and people in the audience threw apple cores and nutshells at him. The good shots hit him in the face. They were big on popular justice, in this century. I'd found out that some crimes were punished by putting people to sit or stand all day in the stocks, with legs or head and hands fastened into a wooden frame, so that anyone who chose could pelt them with rotten vegetables, or dirt, or stones. At the worst, the stones could kill them. I was glad there were no stones handy in the Globe Theatre.

But the boy was in danger all the same. The groundlings at the theater could be a rough lot; they were, after all, the same men and women who loved to watch bulls and bears chained to a pole and attacked by dogs. (And public hangings and beheadings too; Roper was itching to get me to one of those.) By two in the afternoon, the time of the plays, there were always some of them who were drunk. One of these scrambled up onto the stage now: a chunky, short-haired man with a beer belly, and a shirt open halfway down his hairy chest. You could tell he wasn't sober straightaway; he got one leg over the edge of the stage and then fell off, so that the crowd shouted with mocking laughter. But he tried again, and made it; and then he pulled out a dagger and staggered over to the pillar, and the captive boy.

I looked around hastily for Will Shakespeare, but he was gone.

"A pox on all cutpurshes!" shouted the drunk, waving the dagger. Some of the crowd cheered, but others yelled at him to get down. The boy stared at him, terrified, whimpering, straining against the ropes.

The drunk stood in front of him, grinning. He slapped one hand against the pillar above the boy's head, to steady himself, and with the other he put the tip of his dagger against his neck. The boy let out a high gasp of fear. A tiny trickle of blood ran down from the sharp point.

"Wha' shall we do wi' him?" bellowed the drunk to the crowd. They shouted back at him, but in the confusion you couldn't make out any one shout from another. The boy was cringing back against the pillar, wide-eyed, and I suddenly noticed a puddle of water around his shoes; out of sheer stark terror, he had wet himself.

I wouldn't like to guess whether or not the drunk would have pushed his dagger in; I thought he might, and my heart was hammering out of fear for the boy. But at the last minute one of the stage entry doors swung open and out ran two brawny stage-keepers, with Richard Burbage striding behind them in an awesome scarlet cloak. The crowd cheered, in surprise and delight; Burbage was one of their favorites. (The cloak was a cardinal's robe that he had grabbed from a costume rack moments before, I found out later; he wanted to cover his costume as Bottom, which was far from dignified.)

The stage-keepers grabbed the startled drunk, and Burbage snatched his dagger from him. With one great flourishing sweep, he cut the boy's ropes.

"Gentles!" he boomed out. "Pray you, be merciful— this stinking little villain has had his punishment!" He pushed the boy off the stage with his foot, and the groundlings let him scuttle out of the yard, though not without the occasional kick on the way. Master Burbage was still booming, holding their attention. "In one moment only," he cried, "this little drama shall be eclipsed by one far greater—good people, we bring you our play!"

He swept them an elaborate bow, and they roared their affectionate approval. With great dignity Burbage strode off, swinging his red cloak around him, and stage-keepers ran on with mops and brooms to clean the stage, and sweep up the nutshells and apple cores.

As I turned to hurry down to the stage, past the trumpeter who was approaching the gallery to play his opening fanfare, I saw a twitch of curtains in the Gentlemen's Room that overlooked the right-hand side of the stage, and two or three masked faces in the shadows. Unnoticed, with no fuss or danger, under cover of the little drama of the cutpurse, Her Majesty Queen Elizabeth I had arrived to watch our play.

FOURTEEN

I shall never have a day like that again. After the trumpeter's fanfare, sounding out from the top gallery and sending the doves whirling off the roof, I remember very little until my first entrance. I was so nervous, hopping from foot to foot at the back of the tiring-house, that I heard scarcely a word of the first long scene between Duke Theseus and Hippolyta, old man Egeus and the four lovers. I came to my senses only when Master Burbage, as Bottom the Weaver, went bounding onstage with his five fellow mechanicals—and Roper, all white face and red lips as Hermia, came scooting off, holding up his skirts, skidding to a halt at the tiremen's table.

There was a muffled roar from the theater as the audience greeted Burbage again, and Joseph the tireman grabbed Roper and began unbuttoning his dress. Underneath, he wore the floating, gauzy costume of the Fairy: not the kind of pretty-pretty stuff you might expect, but a bizarre, sexless garment that made him an odd little creature—as odd as my Puck. I hoped he knew his words. He and I had to play my first scene together, and because he had been needed for the lovers' rehearsals, we had only gone through it once.

Joseph turned Roper around and attached a pair of

starched gauze wings to his shoulder blades. Roper had
complained about these when the costumes were tried on;
they would get in the way of his tumbling, he said. But
Master Burbage had refused to listen to him.

"Th'art playing a fairy, boy, not a tumbler," he said.
"Fairies have wings."

I was hopping from foot to foot still; I didn't know I was
doing it. A pair of strong hands took me by the shoulders
and pressed down, so that I stopped; then they propelled
me across the dim-lit room to the entrance stage right.

It was Will Shakespeare, wonderfully demonic in his
makeup as Oberon. He said, whispering, "Wait till they
come off, then run on. And speak loud."

I stared up at him, frozen, as Burbage and the rest
came galumphing past us, while the audience laughed
and clapped. He grinned at me, and suddenly everything
was all right, and I ran onstage into that marvelous terrifying bright space ringed by faces. I somersaulted toward
Roper, running from the other side to meet me.

"How now, spirit! Whither wander you?"

"Over hill, over dale
Thorough bush, thorough briar. . . ."

I hoped Will Shakespeare wouldn't think I was over-
doing the somersaults, but the audience liked them, and
Roper and I bounced through our scene, both of us fero-
ciously projecting, until Oberon and Titania stalked on,
mad at each other about who should own the servant boy.
Shakespeare looked magnificent and somehow taller in

his exotic pants and cloak, and as Titania, Thomas was magical, unrecognizable. Master Burbage had given him an amazing multicolored costume that shimmered like a waterfall, quite disguising his pudginess, and his high strong voice rang out like a clarinet.

I don't think they had clarinets, then. Well, Thomas's voice got there first. When that voice broke he would obviously be a clown, because he had that natural comic talent—like the company's new actor Robert Armin, who was playing Flute the Bellows-mender. But today, still a boy, Thomas was beautiful and oddly chilling as the fairy queen. I told him so afterward, and he crowed like a cock and punched me in the stomach.

As for Will Shakespeare, he was King of Fairyland and of the whole world, as far as I was concerned. He wasn't a great actor; he didn't have that indescribable special gift that Richard Burbage had, that could in an instant fill a theater with roars of laughter, or with prickling cold silence. But as Oberon he had an eerie authority that made me, as Puck, totally his devoted servant. When he sent me offstage to look for the magic herb that he would squeeze on Titania's eyes, it was my own delight—me, Nat Field—that put spring into my cartwheeling exit.

> *"I'll put a girdle round about the earth*
> *In forty minutes—"*

And I'd arranged to have the door held open for my hurtling arms and legs, not by Roper, in spite of his repentance, but by Joseph the tireman, who was totally reliable because of his concern for my spectacular green tights.

On we went, through Shakespeare's cheerful chain of misunderstanding and accident, to the scene in which Lysander and Hermia, on their happy way to elope together, lie down to sleep in the wood outside Athens. But it's the same wood in which Puck, sent by Oberon, is hunting for Hermia's admirer Demetrius and his scorned girlfriend Helena.

Instructed by Oberon to make Demetrius fall in love with Helena, I came prowling across the front of the stage, carrying the magic flower.

> *"Through the forest have I gone*
> *But Athenians found I none*
> *On whose eye I might approve*
> *This flow'r's force in stirring love."*

Then I spotted Lysander.

> *"Night and silence—who is here?*
> *Weeds of Athens he doth wear;*
> *This is he, my master said,*
> *Despised the Athenian maid—"*

And I was tiptoeing toward Lysander, flower in hand, when suddenly a piercing voice rang out from the groundlings' yard below me, a girl's voice, full of concern.

"No, no, that's not he—that be the wrong one!"

I stopped, frozen. There was a rumble of laughter from the audience, and a few blurry drunken shouts, and if I'd been reacting as myself, or perhaps if I'd been in my own world and time, I would have been thrown, and spoiled the scene. But I was altogether in Will Shakespeare's time and dream, I was his Puck, and so I reacted as his Puck.

I paused, listening, and cocked my head first to one side and then to the other, as if to say: *Did I hear something?*

The girl called again, urgently—I could see her out of the corner of my eye, a round-faced pretty girl staring up at me, completely caught up in the play—"No, Puck, prithee—he is the wrong man!"

I listened puzzled again to the air, head cocked, and there was a ripple of laughter, different laughter this time, and then I shook my head firmly—*No, of course, I didn't hear anything, I'm dreaming it*—and I squeezed the juice on Lysander's eyes. They really laughed then, a laugh made out of affection for the girl and amusement at me, and they applauded when I ran off.

Nick Tooley, white-painted and robed as Helena, ran onstage past me, to waken Lysander and further screw things up. And Will Shakespeare, who had been watching from the tiring-house door, caught me by the arm as I whirled past him—and then let go hastily, for fear of smudging Burbage's paint. He was smiling. He said, "Th'art a true actor, sprite."

I grinned at him, half out of breath. "Thank you."

He looked me in the eye for one more moment, and it was bright but it was serious. "Promise me never to stop."

"I promise," I said. "I promise."

And I never shall stop.

Then the mechanicals were milling around us, peering at the "plot" for their cue, hissing at the book-keeper to check their lines, and it was time for the scene where they are rehearsing their terrible little play in the wood, and

Puck scares them all to death by changing the head on Bottom's shoulders to the head of an ass.

"Bless thee, Bottom, bless thee—thou art translated!"

Quince says that—big laugh line—before he rushes away after the others.

Master Burbage had a terrific ass's head. The oldest tireman, Luke, was a real whiz at special effects; put him in the twentieth century with computers to play with and he'd have made a lot of money in Hollywood. The head's eyes rolled wildly, on command, and the ears went up and down and sideways. The groundlings loved it. They cheered and shrieked like little children.

The theater was full of shouts and laughter, the play was dancing along. By the time I reached Puck's speech telling Oberon what has happened to Titania, I was high with delight and excitement. There we were, the two of us, at the heart of this happy gathering of three thousand people, at the heart of this fantastical play: together in the center of the stage, Will Shakespeare and me.

"My mistress with a monster is in love—"

Puck is on a high too, in that scene, really full of himself—until Demetrius comes on, pursuing Hermia, and Oberon says, *"Stand close, this is the same Athenian."*

Puck stops still. Uh-oh. He may be in trouble. *"This is the woman, but not this the man. . . ."*

And when Oberon finds out the mistake—

"What hast thou done?" Master Shakespeare thundered

at me, and for a moment it was terrifying to be attacked by that magnificent unearthly presence. But I remembered something he had said to me in rehearsal: "Puck is all mischief," he had said. "He loves jokes, and causing trouble— he has no heart. Don't let him *feel*, like you or me."

So I let the thunder bounce off me, and was wary of Oberon, but not frightened. I was learning things at the back of my head, then, that I had no idea I was learning. Puck danced about, Puck didn't give a darn about real human emotions.

"Lord, what fools these mortals be!"

Puck and Oberon, Oberon and Puck: together we watched and encouraged the lovers' jangling confusions, and Queen Titania's embarrassing love for an ass-headed clod, and then together, pulling the audience with us, we sorted everything out. It was wonderful, playing those scenes in such a theater, like telling a long involved family joke: all around us were friendly faces, intent, enjoying, shouting comments. Yes, they cracked nuts too, and popped bottles of ale open, and chomped on apples, but they came right along with us, all the way to the fairies' dance—Will Shakespeare stepping stately and elegant with Thomas— when Titania and Oberon come together again.

And that was our exit until the end of the play, and we had to slip out through one of the tiring-house exits to make way for the imposing entrance of Duke Theseus and Hippolyta—which, though I didn't know it at the time, was the biggest gamble Burbage and Shakespeare had ever taken in their lives.

I saw them in the tiring-house, Theseus and Hippolyta, poised to go on, and the sight stopped me where I stood. Will Shakespeare was already motionless, watching, as John Heminges, who was Duke Theseus, swept toward the stage in a splendid purple velvet robe and held out his arm to Sam, the husky-voiced senior apprentice who was playing Hippolyta.

It was Sam who was the astounding sight. He wore a gleaming, wide-skirted dress of white satin, embroidered with hundreds of little pearls, and a great winglike embroidered collar rose like a halo behind his head. Above his white-painted, red-lipped face was an elaborate wig of bright red curls; he was the exact image of a portrait of Queen Elizabeth I that I'd seen reproduced on a poster at the new Globe Theatre in my own time.

And that, I realized, was exactly what Burbage and Shakespeare intended him to be. There was even the gold circlet of a crown amongst the red curls.

Shakespeare said softly, "Gloriana."

I could see Sam's hand shaking as he opened his fan. He straightened his back, and with his head proud and high, he swept out into the theater on Heminges's arm. The audience gave a gasp, and voices whispered to and fro, sibilant, muttering. "The Queen . . . She's like the Queen . . ."

Shakespeare was standing very still, listening.

And then they broke into cheers. Spontaneously, all of them, all at once. Perhaps it began as applause for the costume, for the audacity of the portrait, but it swelled at once into an impulsive upsurge of emotion. Those in the galleries, who had been sitting down, jumped to their feet, applauding; the groundlings shouted, "God Save the

Queen!" and threw up their hats. They were all cheering their Queen with as much enthusiasm as if she'd been there in person to hear them.

And she was, of course, though none of them knew that. I looked at the curtain masking the Gentlemen's Room, and half expected to see it flung aside by a jeweled royal hand, but there wasn't a flicker of movement.

Instead, out on the stage, Sam in his queenly costume swept down in a deep curtsy to the entire theater, his hand still resting on Theseus's arm. And then their scene began, Gloriana—the Queen—became Hippolyta, and the audience quieted down.

Beside me, Will Shakespeare let out a long, low sigh of relief.

The book-keeper said softly, "Was tha feared? Really?"

"I feared the serpent's tongue. If they had hissed her, Burbage and I would be headed for the Tower. Headed and headless, like as not."

"They love her," said the book-keeper simply.

"They loved Essex, the other night."

"But this goes deeper."

The lovers came sailing past us and onto the stage, in their proper couples now.

Thomas was close by us, his eyes dark pools in the white Titania makeup. He said to Shakespeare, "You knew they'd not hiss her. You always know what they will do, always."

"I throw the dice, Tom," Will Shakespeare said. "I throw the dice."

And pretty soon after that, Bottom and his fellow mechanicals were on, to perform their play before the court. It's the funniest and best part of *A Midsummer Night's*

Dream, that play—"the most lamentable comedy, and most cruel death, of Pyramus and Thisbe"—and we were all unashamedly crowded near the exit doors, peeking through to watch it. Master Burbage stumped and stamped about as Bottom/Pyramus, with ridiculous stiff gestures and roaring declamation.

> *"O grim-look'd night! O night with hue so black!*
> *O night, which ever art when day is not!*
> *O night, O night, alack alack alack—"*

Shakespeare gave a little soft snort of laughter. "Ned Alleyn to the life," he said.

Guiltily, Thomas giggled. I whispered to him, "Ned who?"

Thomas blinked at me. "Edward Alleyn, of the Admiral's Men. Where do you *live,* Nat? Master Burbage's great rival, until he retired—old Fustian Tamburlaine Alleyn."

"Oh yes, of course," I said hastily—and then luckily the theater exploded into laughter at Robert Armin's entrance in his crudely female costume as Thisbe.

The play-within-the-play rollicked its way through to the staggering, throat-clutching death of the principals. Then there was a comical little clod-hopping dance called a bergomask, danced by two of the actors while another two played—badly—the tabor and drums; then, offstage, a stage-keeper tolled the strokes of midnight on a bell. Theseus broke up the evening, and I heard him speak my cue:

> *"Sweet friends, to bed.*
> *A fortnight hold we this solemnity*
> *In nightly revels and new jollity."*

And off they went and onto the empty stage I stepped, on tiptoe, in my glimmering green tights and my leafy-patterned body, with a broom in my hands, sweeping. I looked out at the audience.

"*Now the hungry lion roars*
And the wolf behowls the moon. . . ."

I could see the faces, all around me, intent now. They'd had done with laughing, they were caught in the last lingering magic of Shakespeare's dream. And so was I. The musicians up in the stage gallery played soft haunting music, a thin white mist crept over the stage from the two entrances, and it all affected me as much as it did the audience. I forgot the frantic stage-keepers who would be puffing away with their bellows at the smoke buckets in the tiring-house. I spoke my speech to the audience, not a cheery speech, telling them this was night now, when out in the dark world, graves gaped open and spirits roved free—and I felt suddenly that a lot of the upturned faces below me in the yard, mouths half open, staring, really believed me. I half believed myself. But here, I told them—

"*not a mouse*
Shall disturb this hallow'd house.
I am sent with broom before
To sweep the dust behind the door."

I turned, to shift their attention to Oberon and Titania moving slowly in with their band of small ethereal fairies, all now with rings of little lighted candles around their heads, to keep watch over the house while its humans slept.

At the back of the stage, Harry and Alex moved unobtrusively in, dressed in white, with three younger boys brought in for the sake of their voices. And I joined them as the whole magical group obeyed Oberon's instruction to dance and sing "and bless this place." I couldn't tell you now the tune or words of the song we sang, but it was slow and soft, rather like a lullaby. I'd know it if I heard it again, though I never have.

When we had woven our way about the stage, and the song was done, a single recorder played softly on in the background under Will Shakespeare's last speech. He stood right in the center of the stage, holding a silver bowl of water, and each fairy came past him and dipped a hand ceremonially into the water as he spoke.

> "With this field-dew consecrate
> Every fairy take his gait
> And each several chamber bless
> Through this palace with sweet peace;
> And the owner of it blest
> Ever shall in safety rest."

Very subtly, as he said those last two lines, he glanced up at the curtained Gentlemen's Room, so that although nobody else would know he was giving his words to the Queen as a blessing, the Queen herself would know. I was so caught in admiration of the simple directness of it that I almost forgot the next two lines were his last, and my cue.

> "Trip away; make no stay;
> Meet me all by break of day."

One by one they tiptoed gracefully away, dividing to go through the two doors. And there I was, left alone on the stage, holding a single candle that at the last moment I had picked like a flower from the headdress of the final departing fairy. Now it was just Puck and the audience, Puck speaking out to each of the three thousand faces all around him, and to the one great creature made out of those three thousand; Puck speaking in the voice of his author.

As Will Shakespeare had told me to do, I said my lines so firmly and clearly that I was almost shouting. I held up my candle, facing the audience on my left, and moved gradually around as I spoke, so that just for a moment every one of them would feel I was looking at him, or her.

"If we shadows have offended,
Think but this, and all is mended.
That you have but slumber'd here
While these visions did appear.
And this weak and idle theme,
No more yielding than a dream,
Gentles, do not reprehend:
If you pardon, we will mend.
And, as I am an honest Puck,
If we have unearned luck
Now to 'scape the serpent's tongue,
We will make amends ere long;
Else the Puck a liar call."

They were dead quiet, listening. With a quick breath, I blew out my candle, and stretched my arms wide to the whole audience.

"So, good night unto you all.
Give me your hands, if we be friends,
And Robin shall restore amends."

For a second I stayed there motionless, until they started to clap and shout, and then I dropped the dead candle and threw myself into one big beautiful cartwheel upstage center, as the company all came running out of the side doors and downstage, to take their bows. Most plays ended with a final dance, but we'd already done ours.

Will Shakespeare reached out as he passed and grabbed my hand, holding it hard, pulling me with him, and we bowed together amongst the rest as the audience cheered and clapped. And that moment above all is what makes me say I shall never have a day like that again.

The musicians struck up cheerful music from the stage gallery, and the audience was still applauding as we all ran out offstage, laughing, thumping each other on the back. There seemed to be no thought of separate star calls, perhaps because there is no one star part in this play. In the tiring-house Master Burbage held up a hand, stood there a moment amongst us, listening, to gauge how long the noise might go on—then grinned and shouted, "Once more!" And back we went, to hear them roar their enthusiasm again. And again.

That third time, when we came back, six large soldiers were standing grouped in the tiring-house, armed and armored and very awesome. With them was the young lord who had visited Will Shakespeare's house two days before. He wore a black velvet doublet and a black silk cloak, and he had pearls in his ears.

He took Shakespeare's arm. "Will—this must be very fast. Her Majesty wishes to see you and Master Burbage. Now, before she leaves." He glanced down at me, and pointed his finger. "And the boy too."

FIFTEEN

There was no time to be nervous. Before you could blink, the soldiers were around us, and we were moving through the crowded tiring-house and out to the nearest stairway, leading up to the Gentlemen's Room. More soldiers stood at every corner, out there; all the corridors and staircases of that part of the theater were cut off. We were an odd sight amongst all the armored breastplates, Richard Burbage in Bottom's ribboned workman's clothes, and Will Shakespeare and I in our glimmer and glitter and fantasy paint.

"Make way!" called the soldier in front of us. "Make way!"

The nameless lord in his black velvet was close beside us as we hurried along. I heard him say close to Burbage's ear, "A master stroke, the Gloriana costume—a master stroke, my dear. Whose inspired idea might that have been?"

Burbage said blandly, "Few things in the theater are one man's idea, my lord."

"As in politics—or at least one should make it seem so." He gave a little snuffling chuckle. "Well, it was a lovely gamble, my dear, and your luck was in. It gave the lady great pleasure."

And then we were there, in the entrance to the crowded little gallery, the air smelling more of perfume than of the garlicky, fusty body smell of the rest of the theater. It was lit by lanterns, because the curtains were still drawn across the front, keeping the gallery from the sight of the groundlings and other more prosperous folk still milling about in the yard below. Past the bending backs of my masters, as they bowed low, I saw the central seated figure, and could hardly take my eyes off her from that moment.

Queen Elizabeth I. She was an old lady. I had expected her to be tall and grand and beautiful, like Sam in his Gloriana costume, but she was not. Only the bright auburn curls of the wig were the same. Underneath it was a wrinkled white face that had lived a long time, with no eyebrows but thin, painted, curved lines, and bright, black eyes like beads, moving constantly, very alert. When she smiled at Burbage and Shakespeare—as she did at once, holding out her hand for them to kiss—she showed badly discolored teeth that would have given my dentist fits.

"Thank you for your *Dream*, gentlemen," she said. "It is a favorite of mine, as you know."

Will Shakespeare said, "Your Majesty is very kind." The antennae on his Oberon head were quivering a little, and I longed to pull them off. They belonged on the stage, not here.

"A gentle play, a merry play," said the Queen, who was sitting back unfazed by antennae, makeup or anything else. "Carrying no political historical baggage. You are a clever fellow, Will Shakespeare, but I have had my fill of the history of my forebears."

Shakespeare said meekly, "The audiences do love a history, Your Majesty."

"I hope you are not writing another."

Burbage said, "A Roman history only, Your Majesty. We have just played Will's tragedy of Julius Caesar."

Elizabeth waved a long finger at them. On several fingers of each hand, she wore enormous jeweled rings. "Enough of the downfall of great leaders, Master Shakespeare. Julius Caesar, and all those senators with bloody hands—it is almost as painful as Richard II giving away his crown."

I couldn't see Will Shakespeare's face, because I was behind him, but his shoulders were beginning to droop. "I beg Your Majesty's forgiveness," he said, rather muffled.

The Queen flashed her terrible teeth at him, and the black eyes twinkled. For an old lady, she had an amazingly flirty way of talking. "Never mind. Thy *Dream* was excellent, and so was thine Oberon." Her gaze flicked over to Master Burbage, standing there stiff and nervous in his leather jerkin with silly little ribbons crossing it. "Dick Burbage, I am pleased to have seen your new theater. The audience was as much an entertainment as the play."

"We are honored by Your Majesty's gracious presence," Burbage said. Everyone seemed to use long stiff words by instinct when they talked to the Queen, as if she wasn't a real person.

"Bottom the Weaver was wonderful tragical-comical. Well done. It was all well done." She looked over his shoulder. "And where is the green boy?"

Some strong hand in my back pushed me forward to

stand between Shakespeare and Burbage, and I bowed so low that my forehead nearly touched my shins.

"Th'art a pretty sight, Puck," said the Queen amiably as I came up, "and a good little player. With a way of speaking that I cannot place—where dost thou come from?"

I stammered out, "St. Paul's School, Your Majesty."

"Wast *born* there?" said the Queen, and she made her eyes so comically wide that I couldn't help grinning.

"No, ma'am. I was born in Falmouth." And so I was. It's a little town in Kentucky, where my parents lived at the time.

"A West Countryman!" said the Queen. "Like my good old pirate Sir Francis Drake." Those beady black eyes peered at me thoughtfully, scarily intelligent. "And thou hast a particularity, a strangeness—wouldst like to be a page at Court, little Puck?"

I said without thinking, appalled, "I am an actor, Your Majesty!" And I guess it came out sounding ridiculous, because they all laughed, though it didn't seem ridiculous to me, just true.

The Queen was smiling. She wore around her neck a thick pleated white ruff, which would have made her head look tiny if it hadn't been for the tall red wig above it. She said to the room in general, "It is a lucky man whose ambition does not vault over his talent."

Then suddenly she had had enough of us. She looked over my head at someone behind me. "Sir Robert?"

I turned to see. An odd, runty little man was standing there, with his head slightly crooked on his neck. But he wore a green satin cloak with a fur collar, and a plumed hat, and he was clearly someone important.

"Your barge awaits, Your Majesty, and the guard is thick-lined to the dock. I shall be glad to see Your Majesty safely homeward bound."

They all started fussing about the Queen as she stood up, and two brightly gowned ladies-in-waiting draped an enormous hooded cape over her shoulders. "You are a fidgety old lady, Cecil," she said irritably, "far more so than I. Did you not hear them cheer their Queen? Or at any rate a wicked replication of their Queen." She patted Master Burbage's arm flirtatiously as she came past him, and she smiled at Master Shakespeare. "The hair a little too red, masters," she said. "A little too red."

Then she was passing me on her way out of the narrow gallery, so that I caught a whiff of perfume, and a hint of a much nastier smell, perhaps from those teeth. "Sweet Puck," she said, "tell thy fellow that the Queen thought him a pretty boy too."

I bowed very low again, and by the time I straightened up, she was gone.

I said to Sam, back in the noisy, hysterical, paint-smelling tiring-house, "She said, *'Tell thy fellow that the Queen thought him a pretty boy.'*"

Sam was still caught under his long skirt, which hung from his shoulders from straps like suspenders. Joseph the tireman was carefully peeling off his pearl-encrusted bodice. "Stand *still*, boy!" he said.

Sam's face was a study in relief and surprise, overlaid by a big pleased grin. "She said that, truly? She wasn't angry?"

Dick Burbage said, swigging from a goblet of wine as he elbowed his way past us, "She said thy hair was too red. Mark that, Joseph."

Joseph paused, looking stricken. "The Queen thought the wig too red?"

"A *little* too red," I said. "And she may have been joking."

"No joke," said Master Burbage, shaking his head with wicked solemnity. "She never jokes about wigs." He took another pull at the goblet, and moved on to join the milling, celebrating company.

Sam said, "A pretty boy?"

Joseph was looking disapprovingly after Master Burbage. He yelled at his vanishing back, "No wine in the tiring-house!"

Sam said again, happily, "A pretty boy. The *Queen!*"

Most of the Chamberlain's Men ended up in the tavern that evening, boys and all. We ate roasted meat and vegetables, and a sticky tart with apples and plums in it, all in the uninhibited greasy way they had of using nothing but fingers and knives. Still, there was a big bowl of water to rinse your fingers, and a napkin to wipe them on. The meat was good; it was mutton, which is like lamb only tougher, and something called coney, which I liked a lot. It was only several months later that I found out a coney is a rabbit.

This was a feast of celebration, because the Master of the Revels, who was in charge of all the Queen's entertainment at Court, had promised the company a performance at the Queen's palace in Greenwich in a month's time. That meant a handsome amount of money, as well as a great deal of prestige. It was to make up for our *Dream*, which carried no prestige because the Queen had been there in secret, and no royal money either, because it had been the Queen's whim not to command us to take our play to her, but to come herself to our commercial theater.

Roper said, "It is a great matter, going to Greenwich, it starts before sunup that day. All the costumes and properties have to be loaded into boats, and taken up to the palace by water." He took a swig of ale, and spluttered noisily with laughter as he suddenly remembered something. "Last time, Thomas fell in the river, and lost his boots."

"That was no joke," Thomas said with feeling. "I got a terrible beating."

Master Burbage had taken over a whole room at the tavern, with a big long table, and we boys were at one end, together. We were only apprentices, after all, to be tolerated but not necessarily heard. It was a musty room, full of good smells and bad. The rushes that were spread everywhere on indoor floors were perhaps changed more often in a tavern than in an ordinary house, because more bits of food and muck fell on them, but even so they were pretty dirty on an average day. Quite often you'd find a mouse or a rat scavenging through them.

As for the people who walked on the floors, I'd begun to realize that hardly anyone in this century except the rich ever took a bath. The more private parts of your body were washed only if you went swimming, in sea or river or lake, or if you deliberately removed all your clothes and washed yourself all over from a basin of water— something that didn't seem to happen often. It no longer bothered me as much as it had in the beginning; maybe I was getting used to body smells, including my own.

I was getting used to a lot of things. I looked down the long table at Will Shakespeare, who was laughing, raising his mug to John Heminges—and suddenly a wave of panic hit me, at the thought of the things that were about to change. I had a very perilous time ahead of me, in which I could no longer be mistaken for· the real Elizabethan Nat Field.

Why was all this happening to me?

Harry splashed some more ale into my mug from the big pewter pitcher. "Why the long face, Nat? Tha met the Queen today!"

I said, truthfully, "I don't want to go back to St. Paul's."

Roper said, "There was a boy from St. Paul's came round to see thee, while tha wast with the Queen. Full of compliments, he was."

I stared at him. "He saw the play?"

"Of course."

"He knew me?"

"A classmate of thine, he said."

"And he really recognized me?"

"Ah well, through all that green paint, who knows . . . Of course he recognized thee, blockhead, he was thy classmate."

For a wild moment I wondered if I might look like a twin of the real Nathan Field. Did Nathan Field have parents here in London? When they saw me, would they instantly know I was a stranger, or—if I did look like him—would they believe me to be their son?

My wonderings got wilder and wilder. Would they look like my real parents? Would they somehow *be* my parents—already dead, yet not to be born for more than 350 years? My memories of my mother were no longer very clear, but the thought of seeing my father again made me shiver with a mixture of excitement and a kind of fear.

Why was all this happening to me?

Roper was staring at me, faintly hostile. "Th'art an odd fish, Nat Field," he said. "Art mad, perhaps?"

"Different," Harry said. "He's different, that's all." He smiled at me, to show he meant no harm.

"Nat is a white witch," Sam said amiably. He made that sign at me, briefly, unobtrusively, the fist with the two pointing fingers, warding off the evil eye. "If we are good to him, he will keep us all from harm."

"And save us all from choking," said Nick Tooley. He thumped Roper on the back. They were all looking at me owlishly, affectionate but a bit wary. It wouldn't have taken much for Roper to have picked a quarrel, but he still remembered that he owed me.

The ale was making us all a bit fuzzy. Looking around the crowded, low-ceilinged room, with its flickering candles and bare plaster walls, I wondered how much longer I could live in this century without trying to do something for it. I might be only a kid, but I knew things they didn't. I could tell them to boil water before drinking it; to keep their food cold so it wouldn't spoil; to keep garbage out of the streets so that it didn't bring the rats, who spread diseases; to brush their teeth . . .

But did I know how to make a toothbrush? No—no more than I knew how to give them electricity or gas or plumbing, radio or television or the telephone. I knew how to use those things, but not how to invent them. I wasn't twentieth-century civilization—I was only a kid.

"What does thy father do, Nat?" said Sam. "Is he a wise man?"

I said, "No. My father is dead."

We straggled home through the dim-lit streets in a gradually dwindling group, walking by way of the Thames jetty to drop off those of the company, like Burbage and Harry, who would cross by boat to the north bank. The river was dark and murky, but a half-moon hung in the sky, scudding in and out of ragged clouds.

Will Shakespeare walked a little unsteadily, with his arm across my shoulders.

"I shall miss thee, little Puck," he said.

In my head a voice screamed: *Then don't let me go! Keep me with you!* I didn't say anything, except a sort of muffled "Mmm."

He said, "I leave very early tomorrow for Stratford. I must see my family, and my father has a lawsuit beginning . . . I shall be gone until Dick Burbage hauls me back again. Which will not be long, I dare say. The carrier will take thee over to St. Paul's at about ten o'clock."

"Thank you," I said miserably.

"Mistress Fawcett has a purse for thee, with twopence for the carrier and ten shillings for thee." He chuckled.

"Do not tell the other boys it is so much, and do not tell Master Mulcaster I gave thee anything at all. The school has been paid already."

"You shouldn't pay me," I said. "I acted for you, not for money."

We had reached the house, and he was fumbling in his pocket for the doorkey.

"We are players, Nat," he said. "We are working men, you and I." He found the key, and had some trouble finding the keyhole. Locks were pretty clunky things then, and his hand might have been stronger if he'd drunk a little less ale. I heard Mistress Fawcett opening the door from the other side.

She paused. "Master Shakespeare?" her voice said, uncertainly.

"The players are returned from triumph, Mistress Fawcett!" Shakespeare said grandly. "Pray welcome us in!"

She had a candlestick in her hand and a funny puffy cap on her head, and she shushed us like two naughty little boys as she opened the door. I guess the neighbors went to bed early in a London where people got up at dawn.

We took off our shoes, and lighted more candles. Mistress Fawcett was wearing a long cotton gown as well as her nightcap, and was clearly on her way to bed. But she paused at the staircase, and looked at Will Shakespeare tentatively. "So she did come?" she said.

Shakespeare turned to her, leaned carefully past her candle flame, and kissed her loudly on her broad cheek. "She came, she was content, she went safely home, she commanded us to play at Court next month—and she told our Nathan here he was a pretty boy."

Mistress Fawcett smiled broadly, nodding at us both like a devoted aunt. "And so he is," she said, and she went off up the narrow stairs, filling the space, her little light disappearing with her.

Shakespeare yawned suddenly: a huge yawn, like a picture I'd once seen of an old lion, full and sleepy after a kill. "I expect to hear of thee, Puck," he said.

I said, "Can I come back? When I finish school—or if things don't go well—can I come back? Please?"

"Of course. Ask and I will take thee. Thou hast a gift that will not break with thy voice—I give thee my promise of a place with the Chamberlain's Men." He reached out one hand and took hold of my chin, tilting my head toward the nearest candle. For a moment he stared at me, the tawny eyes narrowed, thoughtful, puzzled. It was like the way the boys had looked at me in the tavern.

"The Queen saw it too," he said. "The strangeness. My aerial sprite. I shall not forget thee, Nat Field. And thou must remember what my poem tells thee, and be at peace."

If he'd said anything else, I should have burst into tears. I remember I gave a sort of strangled throaty noise and flung my arms around his waist, and hugged him.

He held me close for a moment, and kissed the top of my head. Then he went upstairs, taking his candle and its dancing shadows and leaving darkness behind.

In a blur of unhappiness I went into my bedroom, and sat on the bed for a while, thinking about him. The candle was burning down, guttering, warning me it wouldn't last. I washed my hands and splashed my face from the bowl of water that good-hearted Mistress Fawcett had left there. Then I pulled off my clothes and put on my night-shirt, and got into bed.

The poem Will Shakespeare had given me was under my pillow; I took it out and stared at the angular, difficult handwriting. Tomorrow, I thought, I would work out each word and copy them out privately myself. It was a won-derful poem. Even though I didn't wholly understand it, deep down it had begun to heal the hurt that I'd been try-ing not to look at for the past three years.

I put the crackling paper carefully back under my pil-low, blew out the candle, and lay down to sleep. I wasn't quite as afraid of the next day as I had been, now that Roper had reported on a St. Paul's Boy who seemed to rec-ognize me. Maybe what I was facing wasn't disaster, but more mystery.

And I tried to comfort myself about having to leave Will Shakespeare. After all, he had promised me a place with the Lord Chamberlain's Men; he wouldn't forget me, he wanted me to come back. This was a parting, but it wouldn't be forever.

But it *was* forever.

SIXTEEN

Nathan Field has a dream, lying in his bed that night. It is a summer day, in his dream, with sunlight shafting through green trees, and Nat in the dream is a very small boy, not much more than a baby. His father has his two hands clasped around Nat's body, and he is throwing him a little way up into the air, laughing. He tosses and catches him, tosses and catches. Nat is laughing too; he can hear his own laughter, happy, gurgling.

He looks down—and sees not just his father's bright face but hundreds of other faces, all around them, all looking up, laughing and applauding. And he is no longer among green trees but in a theater, though the blue sky is still there at the top; when he looks up, he can see it through an open circle in the roof.

His father tosses him higher, higher, and a great bird swoops down through the O of the open roof and catches him up, holding his clothes in its beak. Hanging there, rising, he looks down, but he is not frightened. Below him, his father, the rows of faces and the theater itself shrink and disappear, and there is only the misty green of the earth and the blue of the sky, and a wonderful sense of being on his way to a great adventure. A sense of freedom.

But a woman's voice, which he does not recognize, is calling him.

"Nat! Wake up, now! You're leaving today! Wake up, Nat!"

SEVENTEEN

For a moment I thought it was Mistress Fawcett's voice, but then I knew it was a voice I'd never heard before, and I woke to a vague but terrible premonition of change, of unfamiliarity.

"Wake up, Nat!"

As my senses came awake too, there was the feel of a different pillow under my head, a smoother sheet against my cheek, an odd antiseptic sort of smell in the air, a brighter light outside my closed eyelids. It was the second time in my life that I had woken to find myself somewhere I hadn't been when I went to sleep. And so even today, sometimes, I wake in uncertainty, full of fear that when I open my eyes I shall find my reality has been taken away.

The room was filled with daylight, reflected at me from white walls. There were a lot of electric sockets in the walls, with wires running to strange boxes and little screens, and a mysterious red light blinking. I was lying on a bed with a metal frame around all four sides, and beside the bed stood a woman, smiling. She wore white, and she was quite young; her hair was pulled back tightly behind her head.

In panic I shut my eyes again, looking back for the

other side of sleep. My hand crept up underneath the pillow, and groped to and fro, looking for Will Shakespeare's poem, but could find nothing. I sat up abruptly, and picked up the pillow. There was nothing underneath but the bare white sheet.

"Good morning, Nat," said the young woman cheerfully. She pulled down the near side of the bed with a metallic clang, and pressed a button, making the head part of the bed move to a sitting-up angle, with a soft whirring noise. She was smiling at me, with interest but a little warily, I thought. She had a dimple in her right cheek.

"I'm Nurse Jenkins," she said. "Nurse Stevens is off duty, she said she was sorry not to see you again before you go. She sent you her love."

Nurse Stevens? Who was Nurse Stevens? Where was I? "Thank you," I said.

She was busy plumping up my pillows, straightening my bedclothes. "Well, you've had quite a time, haven't you? All this way from America, and we give you this nasty obscure disease. But you're going home this morning. Ten o'clock."

She settled me back against the pillows, as if I were a large doll. I tried to smile at her, and I said "Thank you" again. I was lost. I thought seriously that I might have gone mad.

"Breakfast first," said Nurse Jenkins briskly, and she tugged a bed tray around to jut over my lap. "Then you can have a shower—your clothes are outside the bathroom." She pointed to a door in the corner of the room, and a small suitcase beside it. "Take your time now—

don't rush about. Ring me if you need anything."

She indicated a little buzzer on the bed next to my hand, patted the hand, and turned to go. I said, "Nurse, how long have I been in here?"

"I'm not sure, love, I just got back from holiday. About a week, I think."

She disappeared, and I looked at the breakfast tray. There was a carton of orange juice, with a small plastic glass inverted over it, a carton of strawberry yogurt, a carton of milk, a carton of cornflakes, a paper dish, three little paper packets of sugar. Behind all these was a paper plate holding two bread rolls, two foil-wrapped pats of butter and two tiny foil packs of marmalade, all held together on the plate by a roof of plastic wrap. Wrapped in a small paper napkin were a plastic knife and a plastic spoon. I was looking at the result of four hundred years of progress.

Still, I was hungry, so I ate everything that wasn't plastic, paper or foil.

As I was finishing, Nurse Jenkins dived in and out of the room, leaving a small white bottle on my bed tray. "I brought you some shampoo," she said, looking critically at my head. "I'm really surprised nobody's washed your hair."

Soaping myself in the shower, I was pretty surprised too—at how good it felt to be thoroughly clean again. I washed my hair twice, and toweled it dry and combed it, with a comb I found in a toilet kit in the bathroom. In the mirror I looked like some familiar person whom I'd almost forgotten. I put on clean undershorts, jeans, T-shirt, socks and sneakers, all from the suitcase. I was numb; if I started to think, I would panic.

I can't have left him; I can't really have left him . . .

Nurse Jenkins came back, flashed her dimple, exclaimed over my cleanliness, and began packing into the little suitcase several things I didn't know were mine: the toilet kit, a hairbrush, two paperback books and a silly-looking yellow rubber duck.

"Anything else?" she said, looking around.

I said, "I had a sheet of crackly paper, with a poem written on it. Under my pillow."

Nurse Jenkins pulled the bedclothes apart, looked underneath the bed, shook her head—and then paused as she saw the expression on my face. "It was important, wasn't it?" she said.

I said tightly, "Very, very important."

"I'll copy your address from your chart," she said, and patted my shoulder. She was a plump, comforting person, like a young Mistress Fawcett. "If it turns up I'll make sure it gets to you."

As an afterthought she peered into the wastepaper basket, but found nothing. A tall, lean man in grey shirt and pants came into the room without knocking, pushing a wheelchair. "Nathan Field?" he said.

"That's right, Ali," said Nurse Jenkins.

"Hop in, chum," the man said to me.

"But I'm well," I said. "I don't need a wheelchair."

"Hospital rules, matey," said the man, flashing beautiful white teeth at me. I wasn't used to beautiful white teeth. "You're not better till you're outside the hospital doors."

So I sat in the wheelchair, fully dressed, feeling idiotic, until we reached a waiting room on the ground floor. And there was Mrs. Fisher, and with her was my Aunt Jen, smiling. She took one look at me and started to cry.

They were astounded, they kept saying on the way back to the Fishers' apartment, at how well I looked. Clearly they had expected me to be thin and frail and possibly even weak in the head. This was the first time Mrs. Fisher had seen me since she had—she said—put me in the hospital.

"You were so ill," she said. "Do you remember that night?"

"I remember throwing up," I said. "And I had a fever. I went to bed and you gave me a hot-water bottle."

"That's *all* you remember?"

I remember waking up next morning in Elizabethan England, still Nat Field but a different Nat Field, a boy actor borrowed by William Shakespeare to play before the Queen . . .

"That's all," I said.

"I've never seen such a high fever—I was afraid you'd go into convulsions. So we called the ambulance. You weren't really conscious by then."

Was it all a dream, then, a long elaborate fever dream? Did I never leave this time and place at all?

Mrs. Fisher said, "So we went to Guy's Hospital with you, and next morning they said you had bubonic plague."

I stared at her. I could see Harry's earnest dark eyes looking into mine, in the little bedroom; I could hear him saying in relief, *"Dear Lord, I was afraid you had the plague."* Could *that* have been a dream?

We arrived at the apartment block, and Mrs. Fisher

insisted on carrying my little suitcase. Aunt Jen was clutching my hand, as if I might vanish suddenly away. It was clear they'd had a scary week, but I couldn't get to the point of feeling sympathetic, not yet; I was too deep in my own bafflement about what had really been happening to me.

And in trying to cope with the terrible aching realization that I should never see Will Shakespeare again.

Rachel Levin and Gil Warmun came by, late that afternoon. They both hugged me, and then sat with their eyes fixed on me, in that careful, cautious way people do when you've been ill and they don't want to exhaust you. They brought me a Welcome Back card signed by every member of the company, and a big basket of fruit from Arby, with a note saying I mustn't come back to rehearsal until I really felt strong enough.

"I feel fine," I said. I was trying hard to connect with them, to find my way out of the fog I was in. I couldn't bear the thought that I might have been living a dream.

"He's actually longing to have you back," Rachel said. "He really hopes you can still do Puck. Eric Sawyer is a nice kid but he just isn't up to it, not in that space."

Gil said, "Oberon could use you too. That was one hell of a time to get sick."

The word *Oberon* was like a window opening.

I said, *"Believe me, king of shadows, I mistook."*

"Yeah, I didn't really think you intended to catch the plague. That's taking period realism a bit too far."

"What did it feel like?" said Rachel curiously.

"I can't remember," I said. "It's all a kind of blur. But I'm all right, I'll be at the theater tomorrow." Suddenly I wanted passionately to get back to the Globe. It wasn't my Globe, but it was the next best thing.

Gil stood up. His beard was thickening up; he looked older. "Come at nine, and I'll show you the blocking. There's a run-through at ten." He grinned at me. "Young Eric will fall over with relief. He's been having a hard time with Arby."

"We'll pick you up," Rachel said. "Quarter of nine. Oh, Nat, I'm so glad you're better!" She flung her arms around me and gave me a big extra hug; she was always good at showing affection, Rachel. I wasn't in her world yet, but I tried to hug her back.

Suddenly she let me go, poking an inquisitive finger down the back of my neck, under the edge of my T-shirt. "What's that?"

"What?" I said. I felt her finger rub my skin a little.

"It's paint," she said.

She was holding out her hand, and I saw the fingertip. It was green.

She looked at my neck again, intrigued. "Green paint. And such a neat shape. Look, Gil. Just like a pretty little leaf."

"Must be the hospital," I said. "Some antiseptic stuff." Suddenly sunlight was filling the world, suddenly I was trying not to grin, not to shout. *It wasn't a dream, it wasn't a dream, it wasn't a dream . . .*

*   *   *

I was the only person who knew my life was complicated. To everyone else it seemed very simple: I'd been ill in the hospital, and now I was better and had been released. Since they assumed I'd been lying in bed for a week, often feverish, often asleep, they asked me no questions. All I had to do was listen while they chattered away about what had happened while I was gone, and eat and drink whatever was put in front of me. My aunt and Mrs. Fisher seemed to have become such good friends in the three days Aunt Jen had been in Britain that they worked automatically as a kind of double act, checking my health and strength and appetite, offering me little snacks that I didn't want, patting my shoulder affectionately as they passed.

Claire, the Fishers' daughter, had gone away with friends for two weeks, so Aunt Jen was sleeping in her bedroom. The other Nat Field, or whoever it was in that hospital bed, must have been really ill, because the first phone call to South Carolina had warned her bluntly that there was a chance he—I—might die. By the time she got here the danger was past, but she had clearly been badly scared just the same.

She held me very tightly, when she said good night to me. We've been through a lot together, Aunt Jen and me. She's a high school English teacher, and she was the one who encouraged me to start acting, the year after my dad died. She understood about the comfort you can get from a small separate world, whether it's a theater or a basketball team or the inside of a book.

"Welcome back, Nat," she said. "I couldn't do without you."

"I'm real glad you're here," I said.

And that was true too, in spite of my hopelessness.

There was far more space backstage at the new Globe than there had been at the old one, and it was much cleaner and less drafty. We had four big dressing rooms, with names—Air, Earth, Fire, Water—and real bathrooms with running water and toilets. Behind the stage, instead of hauling furniture up with ropes and pulleys, all you had to do was put them in a big elevator and press a button.

Yet even with all this, I found myself missing the dirt and the smells of the noisy primitive Elizabethan theater, which had so easily become home. I told myself that it didn't matter, that it was what was happening in the theater that mattered, the play and the players, the little separate world. I believed that, but still there was something missing.

I was missing him, of course.

This was Sunday. Monday afternoon would be a preview; on Tuesday *A Midsummer Night's Dream* would open, and run for two weeks, alternating every two or three performances with *Julius Caesar.* Arby had taken me out of *Julius Caesar* because I was supposed to have been so ill; I'd only had bit parts in it anyway. But I was a serious part of his vision of the *Dream,* and that production was far more important to him than my possible state of health. From Arby's point of view, bubonic plague wasn't an extraordinary, life-threatening disease, it was an annoying nuisance that had temporarily screwed up his casting. Back on his stage now, I was an ordinary member of the company and he was the same touchy perfectionist he'd always been. I realized very soon that this wasn't exactly a happy company, because everyone was so jumpy and nervous—but it was a very good one.

Ferdie gave me a big hug when I first saw him. He looked just the same: droopy jeans, long flapping T-shirt, three chains around his neck.

"Welcome back to the human race, my man!"

"How you been, Ferdie?"

"Stressed. Arby stress. He got us running like little hamsters on a wheel."

"He'll be better now you're back," little Eric Sawyer said. He punched me on the arm, his smile as bright as his red hair. "He was worried. We all were."

"I'm just fine," I said, and tried to believe myself. "I'm just fine."

Before rehearsal, Gil walked me through our Oberon-Puck scenes on the stage. It was eerie, because so many of the moves were the same as those I'd played with Will Shakespeare—especially, of course, the acrobatic exits and entrances I'd taken into the past with me, which had been invented by Arby four hundred years after they were played. I couldn't get my head around the time difference; it was as if I were living in both centuries at once. On stage in particular, I kept waiting for Roper and Harry to come on, or John Heminges, Henry Condell, Dick Burbage . . .

And instead of Will Shakespeare I had Gil. I suppose he was actually a better actor than Shakespeare, both technically and intuitively, but it wasn't the same. I was like a planet that has lost its sun. Our scenes together didn't have the personal connection they'd had when he and I had played together before, and Gil could sense it, and was puzzled. He knew we'd lost something. He probably hoped it would come back in performance.

I hoped so too, but not enough to try to do anything about it. I was still pining. I wasn't really there. When I went off to put a girdle round about the earth in forty minutes, this time I wasn't a spirit in love with his master, but an obedient little servant. I felt as if I were inside a huge thundercloud, waiting for the storm to explode.

When I first bumped heads with someone, it wasn't with Gil, but with the designer, Diane, who had just flown in from New York for a few days. She hovered while Maggie the wardrobe mistress put Gil and me into our costumes; then she nodded her head in approval.

"It all looks great. The lightness really sets them off against the others."

Oberon, Titania, the fairies and I were all dressed in Elizabethan costume, in assorted shades of white and cream. I looked at Gil's formal creamy brocade cloak, and my puffy white pants and white legs, and I hated them. I said, "It's all wrong!"

Diane looked down at me as if she'd heard a mouse bark. She was a tall, lean lady with bright red nails and long dark hair, and she wore long floaty black clothes and lots of jangly jewelry. She said dangerously, "What did you say?"

"They wouldn't have looked like that!" I said.

Diane sighed. "It was common for Elizabethan plays to be done in Elizabethan costume," she said.

"But not this one!" I said.

Diane smiled at me, with some effort. "Well, Nat, since neither of us was there when they did it, I'm afraid you're just going to have to put up with what you've got."

"You look lovely," said Maggie, pacifying me. "Like a snowflake."

I said, "I look like a vanilla ice-cream cone."

"Well, try not to melt onstage," Diane said nastily. She turned to Gil, who was trying to pretend he was somewhere else, and she began adjusting his cloak.

I stared at myself sulkily in the mirror, and tried not to think about Master Burbage's wonderful green leaves.

I found the run-through a very painful business. Here I was, straight out of Will Shakespeare's own fresh new *Midsummer Night's Dream,* trying to adjust to Arby's production, which was designed to shake up four hundred years of familiarity, not to mention the accumulated boredom of generations of kids forced to read it only on the page. I had to bite my tongue as we went along, to stop myself shouting out warnings of how a line would work or not work. Once or twice I said things anyway, and this was not popular. The company were all supposed to know this theater better than I did, not the other way around.

Arby must have been taken aback by the erratic behavior of quiet Nat Field, his athletic but shy Puck from Greenville, South Carolina. He wasn't to know that someone who starts off quiet and shy can be turned into a kind of simmering volcano, if he's flung in and out of the past, and given more emotions to cope with in a week than some people have in a lifetime.

Our real explosion came over that exit line when

Oberon sends Puck off to get the magic herb; when, for Will Shakespeare, I had cartwheeled my way upstage and all the way off. When the line came this time—

> *"I'll put a girdle round about the earth*
> *In forty minutes—"*

—instinctively I threw myself into the first cartwheel, and at once Arby's voice boomed out from the gallery where he was sitting.

"NO, Puck! Exit through the house, remember!"

I stopped, and looked toward the gallery; I couldn't see him properly.

"It's better this way!" I called out.

He ignored me. "Jump down, without hitting a groundling—run out through the yard door, and around back."

I stood obstinately still on the stage. "Shakespeare hated exits through the theater!" I shouted at him.

Arby rasped, "Just do what I ask, Nat."

"He did, he thought they were corny!"

"And who gave you that little gem?"

"I just know it!" I longed passionately to be able to yell, *He told me so, you idiot!*

Arby was angry now; he had all the weight of two productions on his mind, and I guess he wasn't going to be crossed by one little actor. His voice began softly, and it rose and rose. "Whatever William Shakespeare may be said to have preferred, Nat, I want you to run forward, jump down and run out, as we rehearsed—you may have been sick, but you can still take direction, and I am alive and kicking and directing this show for this century and *Shakespeare is dead!*"

It was just about the worst thing he could possibly have chosen to say, and it hit me like some terrible bolt of lightning. Sure, I knew Will Shakespeare was dead—he'd been dead for nearly four hundred years—but two days ago, for me, he had been alive, warm and alive and hugging me, promising me a place as an actor in his company. I loved him and I missed him, and I should never see him again, never, never, never, never, never—

Something in my mind fell apart. I looked out at the gallery and shouted my line, to Arby, not to patient Gil standing there on the stage.

> "I'll put a girdle round about the earth
> In forty minutes—"

I heard my voice crack on the last word, and I leapt down from the stage and ran out across the groundlings' yard and through the exit door, crying, and I kept on running, out and away and up the street, toward the River Thames, which flowed on fast and grey-green and unchanging, just as it had last week, just as it had four or forty centuries ago.

Gil came after me, and Rachel with him. She'd been sitting up in the gallery with Arby and he'd sent her, instantly, though I didn't know that for a while. I was in costume and so was Gil, and we must have looked pretty stupid running through the streets of London. But the Globe is a busy place, with tourists flocking through it constantly, so we might have been mistaken for a staged bit of local color. I had to thread my way through a crowd on the jetty near the theater, a whole class of French schoolchildren with teachers yelling at them in French. I guess that was what slowed me down enough for Gil and Rachel to be able to spot me and follow.

I ran blindly, along the Thames, up a lot of steps to Southwark Bridge. A big cruise boat swept by on the river, with a blurred voice booming from it. Over the glass and concrete and brick buildings on the opposite bank rose the great dome of St. Paul's Cathedral, where there had been a different church altogether in Shakespeare's day. In my day, my other day. Southwark Bridge hadn't been there then either, nor any of the other bridges I could see through the green and yellow railings as I ran.

But I wasn't paying attention to bridges; I was dodging through puzzled people, running in my white Elizabethan costume, crying. Then I was across the river, turning into a narrow cobbled street under a sign that read SKINNERS LANE, and it was there that Gil and Rachel caught up with me.

Rachel grabbed me and put her arms around me, and I sobbed into her shoulder and she rubbed my back. Just for a minute or two. Then I tried to pull myself together. Gil gave me a fistful of tissues, and squeezed my arm.

"I'm sorry," I said, snuffling through the tissues.

"It's all right, it's all right," they said, in several different ways, and Rachel started to explain how Arby was very stressed out and hadn't meant to upset me, and how he thought I was a wonderful little actor, and all that sort of stuff.

I said, "Can we sit somewhere for a while?"

"As long as you want," Gil said.

So we went back around the corner to Southwark

Bridge and found a bench, set back in the sidewalk under a curlicued wrought-iron lamppost, and up there over the Thames with the taxis and buses rumbling past us, I told them everything there was to tell.

EIGHTEEN

They sat there staring at me. The sun shone briefly out of the bustling clouds overhead, and glimmered on the little diamond in the side of Rachel's nose.

Gil said to me slowly, "You are so *lucky.*"

"Wow, Nat," Rachel said. "Oh wow!"

For a moment they were quiet again, just looking, thinking, imagining.

I said, "I was afraid you'd say it was all a dream."

Rachel laughed, and shook her head.

"Of course not," Gil said. Sitting there in his Elizabethan doublet and his beard, he looked a little like a younger version of Shakespeare. "How could anyone have such an incredibly long dream? And there's stuff in there—people, details—that you couldn't possibly have picked up just from reading, specially not at your age."

Rachel said, "And there's the leaf."

"The leaf?" he said.

"The painted green leaf on the side of Nat's neck, remember? Left from his Puck makeup. I touched it. Some paint came off on my finger. My Lord. I touched paint that *Richard Burbage* painted on him four hundred years ago."

"Two days ago," I said.

"Is it still there?"

"I tried to keep it, but it must have rubbed off on my T-shirt."

"Keep the T-shirt!" Rachel said, excited. "Someone could analyze the paint, show that it was old. Carbon dating, or something."

"No," I said. "I don't need that." I felt suddenly very tired, drained of energy. My head ached, and my eyes were puffy from crying. I stared out at the fast-flowing, grey-green river, where a small, tough tug was trying to tow an enormous barge upstream. I said, "All I want to know is, *why has all this been happening to me?*"

"The other boy," Gil said. He gave a cold look to a pair of teenage girls, giggling at his costume as they passed. "The boy who was in the hospital here sick, when you were healthy in the past. Who was he?"

"Another Nat Field. Nathan. That was his name too."

"Where's he gone?"

"Back where he came from, I guess. We must have swapped. And nobody was able to tell. Nobody who knew me was allowed near him in the hospital here. And at the old Globe, the only person who'd have known I wasn't him was Will Kempe—who walked out just as I arrived."

"Nat Field—we have to find him!" Gil said. He jumped up, pulling Rachel with him.

"That's dumb," I said wearily. "How can we possibly find him? He's gone back in time."

"Get up," said Gil. He grabbed my arm. "We're going to find him in the record books. We'll start with the books in Arby's house, and Rachel will get us a sandwich, and maybe we'll go back to the theater and maybe not."

"Actors!" Rachel said, and rolled her eyes. "Cast them

as a king and they think they can behave like one."

Gil ignored her. He put his hands on both sides of my face, cupping it, and looked me in the eyes for an instant. "Nat—everything's going to be all right."

Nothing was ever going to be all right, but it was nice of him to try.

We went to the house that Arby was renting; Rachel had her key on a chain around her neck, along with a little grey stone with a hole in it, from some special beach she loved in Northern California. Julia wasn't there; like everyone else, she was at the theater getting ready for our opening. I suppose I should have felt guilty that I wasn't there, but I didn't. I didn't know how to feel involved in the way I had before.

Rachel took us to the room Arby was using as a study—which actually was a study, belonging to the house's owner, a lecturer at London University who was spending the summer in Australia.

The room was full of bookshelves and books and piles of papers. Rachel made a beeline for a small tower of books on the floor next to the desk. "These are Arby's, he's been going mad buying books at the Globe shop. Specially some guy called Andrew Gurr, who writes about the Elizabethan theater. Arby thinks he's God."

"I've seen those," Gil said. He dropped on his knees next to her, and pretty soon all three of us were on the floor, each flipping through a book. I don't know whose voice came first, Gil's or mine.

"Nathan Field!"

"Nathan Field!"

"He's here too," said Rachel, from her book, "but it calls him Nathaniel."

Gil was peering at the bottom of a page. "He did go to St. Paul's School—that's what you said, Nat, right? It says, in 1596 Richard Mulcaster became High Master at St. Paul's School, and while he was there he taught Nathan Field, the Blackfriars Boys' best player."

"Mulcaster!" I said. I heard Will Shakespeare's voice in my head. "*Richard Mulcaster has of his kindness lent us his Puck. You.*"

Gil looked up at me quickly. "Did you meet him?"

"Shakespeare said he was my teacher."

"And that was in 1599. It fits."

"The Blackfriars Boys were later than that," Rachel said, turning pages. "A year later—1600. Nathan Field was their star."

"So in 1599 he spends a week in the twentieth century, which maybe he hardly notices because he's so ill, and the next year he leaves school and joins the Blackfriars Boys Company. Goes from acting in school plays to being a pro."

"But before that—" I said. I was hunting urgently through my book to find out whether I—no, not me—whether Nat Field went back to Will Shakespeare's company, to the Lord Chamberlain's Men. Surely he must have gone back, how could he not have gone back? But I couldn't find anything. Why not? He, we, couldn't have stayed away from him for long—

I reached for Gil's book instead, frantic to know what happened. I was a crazy mixture of emotions by now, fiercely jealous of the first Nat Field for having gone back to the world and the people I'd had to leave; passionately concerned to make sure that he'd done the right things afterward, the things I would have done.

Gil clutched his book. "Hey, hold on."

I said urgently, "I can't find when he went back to Shakespeare's company."

Rachel reached out and took hold of my arm. She said, "But, Nat, he was never in Shakespeare's company. You were. He was here."

I stared at her. She let go of my arm, and patted it, and smiled at me, that hopeful kind of smile that doesn't know if it's managing to reach its target.

She was right, of course. My first day in that century had been the day Nat Field and Will Shakespeare first met. My last was the day Nat Field left the Globe to go back to St. Paul's School. But that Nat Field wasn't him—it was me.

I couldn't get my head around it; all I could see was Shakespeare. I said, "But he said I could go back later on, he said I could have a place in the company."

"He was talking to *you*, honey," Rachel said gently. "The other Nat Field didn't want that, he didn't even know Shakespeare, he wanted to be with the Blackfriars Boys."

It was me. Yes, it was me, not him. I was the one he rescued from the pit I was in. But why have I had to lose him?

Gil was looking at another page. "Hey, he did well, the other Nathan. He was their star actor for years, he grew up in the company and he wrote plays too. And poetry."

"This book calls him a 'major playwright,'" Rachel said.

I turned to the next reference in the book I had—and suddenly there was a face on the page, and the caption read NATHAN FIELD.

It was a black-and-white reproduction of a painting: a young man in his twenties, with a rather delicate, fine-boned face, and a pearl earring dangling from the only ear you could see. He had wide dark eyes, long curly dark hair, a moustache and a hint of a beard. He was wearing an expensive-looking, embroidered shirt, and holding his right hand over his heart. He didn't look even remotely like me.

On the opposite page was a painting of Richard Burbage. He looked older than the Burbage I knew—a bit like Arby with a beard—but otherwise it was a lot like him. The caption said it was "thought to be a self-portrait." He was looking straight out at me from the page, and that made me feel very weird indeed.

Rachel and Gil were peering over my shoulder. Rachel said, "Look at this. 'Nathan Field died a bachelor with a considerable reputation, of the kind not uncommon among players, for success with women.'" She chuckled, and prodded my back.

Gil wasn't paying attention, he was studying another paragraph. "It says he was in the King's Men for the last four years of his life. There you go, Nat—that was Shakespeare's company."

"Shakespeare's company was the Lord Chamberlain's Men," I said.

"Only till the Queen died. When James I came to the throne, he made them the King's Men." Gil was back at his own book, flicking through. "Here it is—Nathan Field joined the King's Men as an actor-writer in 1616 or so."

Rachel said, "That was the year Shakespeare died."

"Shoot," I said. That made me really depressed. I'd wanted there to be a connection between Will Shakespeare and my namesake. It wouldn't make any difference, it didn't make any sense, but it would have been a tiny thing to hang on to, even though Nathan Field and I shared nothing but our name.

"But there's something else," Gil said. "Those companies were all owned by the top actors—each of them had one share, except Burbage, he had more. And you know what? Nathan Field bought Shakespeare's share."

I got up off the floor and went over to the window. The sky was grey, and so was the city, and the river. Okay, so I had my link between Field and Shakespeare now, I had all these dates and figures, but all I felt was the huge ache of separation. I'd been given such a wonderful present, the best thing to have happened since my father died, and then it had been taken away.

Rachel came and put her arm over my shoulders.

I said miserably, "But why? *Why* did it all happen?"

Gil said, "I've been thinking about that." He was sitting there cross-legged on the floor, still in his Elizabethan costume of course; he looked like a portrait himself. "I think it must have been the plague."

"The plague?"

"Nathan Field had bubonic plague. If you got the plague in those days, you died. But if you get it today, they can cure you quite easily, if they catch it soon enough. With antibiotics. *You were switched with Nathan Field so that he could be cured of the plague.*"

I stared at him. "Who switched us?"

"Ah, that's another question," Gil said. He shrugged.

"Time. God. Fate. Depends what you believe in."

"Nathan Field wasn't so very special, to have that happen. None of us had ever heard of him."

"It wasn't done for Nathan Field," Gil said. His eyes looked very bright, as if he were suddenly high.

"Oh my Lord!" said Rachel. She turned to him. "Shakespeare!"

Gil nodded. He was grinning.

"It was 1599, Nat," Rachel said. "Shakespeare was only in his thirties, he wrote most of his greatest plays after that. If he'd acted with Nathan Field instead of with you, he'd have caught the plague and died."

"We wouldn't have had *Hamlet* or *Othello* or *King Lear* or a dozen others," Gil said. "We'd have lost the best playwright that ever lived. You may feel you've lost him, Nat, but you saved him. If you hadn't gone back in time, William Shakespeare would have died."

It was true, I guess; if there was a reason for the time slip, that was it. Realizing it should have knocked me sideways.

But it didn't, not then. Whether Will Shakespeare had been in his thirties or his fifties when he died, the fact remained that he was dead. Like my mom, like my dad. I didn't have long enough with any of them. And Shakespeare was so clear in my mind, he'd flashed through my life like a shooting star such a little while ago; I couldn't bear to let go of the image of him alive and unpredictable, of the sound of his voice, the sight of that quick smile brightening his face.

I dropped to the floor next to them again. I said, swallowing to keep the misery out of my voice, "He gave me a poem. He copied it for me, after I'd told him about my dad dying. He wanted me to keep it so it would help. I put it under my pillow, but"—I choked up, and thumped my fist on the floor to make myself go on—"but then I woke up in the hospital, and it was gone."

Gil said, "Was it one of the sonnets? D'you remember any of it?"

I tried, but I'd only heard it the once, when Shakespeare read it for me. "There was something about marriage in the first line. And further on it said that love was an ever-fixed mark."

Gil and Rachel looked at each other, a quick private look.

Gil said quietly, "We can find that for you."

Rachel got up, and fetched a book from one of the shelves behind the desk. It was a big fat *Complete Works of Shakespeare*. She gave it to Gil, and sat down cross-legged beside us.

Gil opened the book near the back, and flipped through pages of sonnets, until he paused. He said, "Number one sixteen," and he began to read it aloud.

> *"Let me not to the marriage of true minds*
> *Admit impediments—"*

From the doorway, a deeper voice said,

> *"—Love is not love*
> *Which alters when it alteration finds*
> *Or bends with the remover to remove.*
> *O no! It is an ever-fixed mark*
> *That looks on tempests and is never shaken—"*

It was Arby. Standing there, casually, one hand in his pocket, he went right through the poem to the end, in that deep actor's voice of his, reminding me suddenly of Master Burbage's voice, and when he'd finished I saw Gil and Rachel were unobtrusively holding hands. I glanced away fast, so as not to embarrass them.

There was a silence for a moment, and then Arby gave us a little crooked grin. He said, "Thought you might be here. I came home to grab a sandwich, and to find my Puck." He turned and went off down the hallway toward the kitchen.

Gil stood up. "I'll be back," he said. He leaned over and gave Rachel and me a squeeze on the shoulder, one hand on each, and went after Arby.

Rachel said, "You still have your poem, Nat."

"I guess so," I said. I looked at the page, and felt slightly better. "I do, don't I?"

"I think I know why he gave you it," she said. "Specially if it was after talking about your father. It's a wonderful poem. It says, loving doesn't change just because someone isn't there, or because time gets in the way, or even death. It's always with you, keeping you safe, it won't ever leave you."

"*An ever-fixed mark,*" I said.

Rachel nodded. "*Even to the edge of doom.*" She looked down at the page, and then across at me. "You met him!" she said softly. "You *spoke* to him!"

Then suddenly she got up, pulling me with her. "Let's go eat lunch. Are you coming back to rehearsal? We open tomorrow."

I said reluctantly, "It's so hard playing it, after everything."

"I know. But if he gave you a poem, I figure you can give him a performance. Even if it's not the same as the one you did with him. What do you think?"

"I'll let you know," I said.

NINETEEN

In the kitchen, Gil and Arby were making tuna fish sand-wiches and talking about Titania's little unseen serving boy in *A Midsummer Night's Dream*, the one she and Oberon fight about. This had always been a sore point with Rachel, who was permanently pissed off that Titania gives way in the end, and lets Oberon take the boy, in spite of all the good reasons she's given earlier in the play for being attached to him. Pretty soon there was a brisk, though quite friendly, argument going on about antifemi-nist stereotypes, or something like that. It suited me fine. I ate my sandwich and sat quietly on the edge of the con-versation. I was feeling totally numb.

But I went back to rehearsal. What else was I going to do? Arby had brought me from the United States to play Puck, that was my job. And Rachel was right: Will Shake-speare had given me a poem, so I owed him a perfor-mance—a second performance. Most important of all perhaps, I was an actor, I wanted always to be an actor, so the Globe Theatre—and all other theaters like and unlike it—would always be my world.

Just before we left the house, I slipped back into Arby's study. I wanted to copy out my poem, so that I could keep it with me. I had the big *Complete Works* open on the desk, and I was scribbling hastily on a piece of scrap paper, when Arby came into the room and saw me.

He came to the desk and looked at my paper. He didn't say a thing at first, he didn't ask me what I was doing or why; he simply reached down to the pile of books on the floor beside the desk, did a little excavation and pulled out two slim paperbacks.

"This is for you," he said, and he handed me one of the books. It was a copy of Shakespeare's *Sonnets*.

I was startled. "Uh—thank you," I said. "Uh—are you sure you—"

"I have a bunch of copies," Arby said. He handed me the other paperback. "Do you know this one?"

The title said *The Tempest,* by William Shakespeare.

"No," I said.

He said, "Take it. You should read it sometime. Better still, see it acted, if you're ever in the right place."

"Why?" I said.

"You'll know why," Arby said.

Then we went back to the Globe, and I forgot all about *The Tempest* in the pressure of rehearsing the *Dream*. But I didn't forget about my poem.

I slept like a log that night. I was worn out by all the emotion, not to mention the rehearsing. They had it all down pat, it was a very smooth production by now. Things weren't like that in my day—in Shakespeare's day, I mean—when there simply wasn't time to rehearse so much. Every performance had its awkwardnesses and thribblings.

My day. What was my day? Which side of the four-hundred-year gap?

This *Dream* was going to look and sound gorgeous; I had to admit that, once I'd reconciled myself to seeing on the stage the clothes I'd seen on the streets only days before. Arby had taken great pains with every detail. Even the music sounded just like what I remembered—not the exact tunes, but the sound of it, the kind of instruments the musicians played.

I was due at the Globe at ten in the morning for our two o'clock opening performance. Mrs. Fisher had gone to work by the time I got up, though she was taking the afternoon off to see the play. I ate a huge breakfast; Aunt Jen cooked me two fried eggs and some thick, meaty English bacon. We'd already done all our catching up with news from home; we were just comfortable together. I reread my poem while I ate—Aunt Jen wasn't one of those people who ban books from the table a hundred percent of the time—and looked at some of the other sonnets. There was one couplet I liked a lot:

> *So long as men can breathe or eyes can see,*
> *So long lives this, and this gives life to thee.*

"Thee" was the person he was writing the poem about, but it seemed to me that it could also mean him, Shakespeare. Even though he'd been dead for almost four hundred years, here we were still acting his plays, reading his sonnets, as if he were alive.

I just wished I could find that comforting.

Aunt Jen said, right out of the blue, "I wish Gabriel could see you this afternoon. He'd have been so proud."

Gabriel was my father.

I felt my eyes fill with tears, before I'd even had time

to think—but they were good tears, somehow, better than the dry pain that I'd had for so long.

She put a hand on the back of my neck. "I'm sorry, honey, I didn't mean to upset you."

"You haven't," I said. "I wish he was here too."

"He's been on my mind a lot this past week," she said. "We never talk about him, do we? I think we shall, more often, now you're getting older." She sat down opposite me. She was wearing jeans and a white shirt, with a Navajo turquoise ornament on a chain around her neck; she looked rather like a kid, except for the grey ponytail. She said, "Do you remember him well?"

"Not as well as I used to. I remember little-kid things, like him throwing me up in the air and catching me, when I must have been really young. I remember him reading to me, at night when I was in bed. Aunt Jen—I'd like to read his poems."

"They're all waiting for you at home," she said. "They're difficult—but if you can manage the Sonnets, you can try him. You'll find yourself in a few of them."

"Really?"

She picked up my paperback. "Poets find truth by writing about what they love," she said.

"Did he say that?"

Aunt Jen laughed. "No—I just said it. Your father and William Shakespeare say things better than that." She looked at her watch. "You should leave soon—I'll walk you to the theater. Mustn't keep Mr. Babbage waiting, not today."

I said blankly, "Who?"

She blinked at me. "Your director, of course."

I sat very still. I said, "We're so used to calling him Arby, I guess we forget his other name."

"Arby," said Aunt Jen with mild interest. "The initials, I suppose. RB. Richard Babbage."

I thought about that name, and those initials, all the way to the theater. It was a weird echo, and it spooked me out. But I didn't take it any further, not then. The moment I was back with Arby, it went out of my head. He was so much his very positive self, so firmly planted in the theater of today and his own ideas about what it should be like.

There was always something about the way Arby dressed that told you he had to be an actor, or a director, or maybe a painter. It wasn't that he looked outrageous, he just never looked ordinary. Quite often he was dressed all in black. Today, as a tribute to the opening, he wore black jeans, a purple shirt open at the neck, and a gold medallion around his neck.

He was also being extremely irritable, rehearsing Gil, Alan Wong, Eric, me and four other "fairies" onstage in the dance that hallows the Duke's house at the end of the play. He had a group of English musicians up in the gallery, and couldn't get their tabor player, who was also their leader, to give him the tempo he wanted. By the time they got it right, the smaller fairies were beginning to fool around at the back of the stage. One boy in particular was being obnoxious, trying to start a belching contest, ignoring all warnings. After the loudest belch, Gil flicked a finger sharply against the side of his head, and the kid shrieked as if he were being murdered. And Arby blew.

"*Warmun*—you just touch one of those kids again, and I'll have you out of this play faster than light! Are you crazy? People who hit children end up in jail!"

I was so indignant on Gil's behalf that I made the huge mistake of shouting back at him. "It was the kid's fault, not Gil's!"

"Keep your mouth shut, Field!" Arby snapped.

"You didn't see what was happening! Leave him alone!"

"Shut up!"

"Shut up yourself!" I shouted. I could feel Gil's hand gripping my shoulder, but it was no good, I couldn't stop. I was so angry with the world, with everyone and everything—and now suddenly the rage had found an outlet and there was no way to stop it pouring out. "You think you're God!" I shrieked at Arby. "You have to be right all the time, don't you, you won't let anyone else have feelings, it's all you, you, you! Who do you think you are?"

I was screaming at him like a mad person, and everyone on stage was standing frozen, staring at me. I heard the shrill echo of my voice curve around the theater as I stopped.

There was a moment's stunned silence, and then Arby said from the stage gallery, "Everyone take a ten-minute break in the greenroom. Or get into costume, if you aren't already." His voice was calm and level now. "Keep those small children under control, Maisie. Nat Field, I want to see you up here. Now." His eyes shifted briefly to Gil. "Alone."

Everyone quietly moved away, out through the stage exits to the big backstage doors, which led to parts of the theater that hadn't been there in my other Globe. Gil rubbed my back for an instant and went away; we both knew there was nothing he could do. I hadn't really been yelling because of him, I'd been yelling because of me.

I went up to the gallery. The musicians' chairs were grouped there, a music stand in front of each, and Arby was sitting in one of them with his back to me.

For a moment I felt a kind of giddiness, and I put out a hand to the wall to steady myself. In the air, from the wooden O of the roof, I could hear the burbling of the doves that I'd heard four hundred years ago, loud, very loud, growing louder.

Arby didn't move. His broad shoulders looked different suddenly, yet still familiar, and my neck prickled with uncertainty. He turned his head, and there he still was, the same face, with the long chin and the rather big nose, but with a look of someone else too.

"Sit down, Nat," he said quietly. "I didn't intend to have this conversation, but there's no way to predict how fast a wound will heal. Or how slowly. And you have your deep cut right on top of the old scar, and so you scream."

I sat down on one of the musicians' chairs. I suddenly felt he knew far, far more about me than I knew about him. It was like being on the edge of a precipice and trying not to look down. "What do you mean?" I said.

"It's cruel, isn't it?" Arby said. "You lost your father, in that terrible way, and part of you froze into a little ice block, like the heart of the Snow Queen. Then a man from the past warmed you to life again, and before you could blink, you lost him too. Time took him away. Cruel, cruel."

How did he know about my father? I'd never told him. *How did he know about Will Shakespeare?*

"Has Gil talked to you?" I said.

Arby paid no attention. He wasn't listening to me. "We think too much about past and present, Nat," he said.

"Time does not always run in a straight line. And once in a while, something is taken away in order that it may be given back."

He got to his feet, and stood there looking down at me, in his purple and black. The light glinted on the medallion around his neck, drawing my eyes like a hypnotist's finger. It was as if he had taken us both out of the real world and we were up in the sky, in space, looking down at it. Looking down at the blue planet that the astronauts see. Looking at all the centuries, all the things that happen and are so hard to explain or understand.

That was the picture that came into my head, just for that moment, and I swear he'd put it there.

Arby reached out and took my hand. He said, "An American actor called Sam Wanamaker spent half his life making a dream come true, making it possible for Shakespeare's Globe to be rebuilt in this place. So it was built, and here it is. The place where Nat Field could be brought to Nat Field. But not by accident."

The hair was beginning to prickle on the back of my neck again.

"Will Shakespeare had to be saved," Arby said. "Once the Globe was here, I had my own work to do. To form a company of boys. To choose the right play, and arrange for it to be played at the Globe. To find and cast a boy whose name was Nat Field, who had a fierce painful need strong enough to take him through Time."

I was staring at him. I must have looked like a frightened rabbit. I said, "Who are you?"

"Just an actor," Arby said. He let go my hand. "Richard Babbage, from London via Massachusetts, at your service."

But he slurred the word a little, in his English-American accent. There was no knowing whether he had actually said "Babbage"—or "Burbage."

The doves were cooing in the roof.

"Everything is repaired, everything is healed," Arby said. "Nat Field was made well, Will Shakespeare lived to give us his plays. But a part of you is still wounded, still angry, so there is one more thing I must tell you, to bring the healing full circle. I think Will missed you, Nat. He missed his Puck, his aerial sprite, when the sprite went to St. Paul's and never came back."

I thought: *I miss him too. Oh I miss him too.*

He was looking down at the stage, this man we called Arby. He was in profile, half shadowed, unreadable.

I was sitting very still; I hardly dared breathe.

"And though he had lost you, I think he kept the memory of you in his head," he said. "Toward the end of his life, when he was writing little, and acting less, he wrote one more great play, and he wrote you into it." He looked across at me. "Do you remember what he used to call you?"

I heard that warm, velvety voice in my memory. *Th'art a sprite, an aerial sprite, born of the air. One day I shall write thee an airier Robin Goodfellow—unless thou leave me, or grow old . . .*

I said, "Like you said. He called me his Puck. His aerial sprite."

He smiled. "That play I gave you to read, *The Tempest*. It's about a great magician, called Prospero. Will Shakespeare played him, a few times—it was the last part he ever played. And in the play, Prospero has a servant, a spirit, a sort of ethereal Puck, whose name is

Ariel. No doubt a good little actor played him, a pretty light-footed boy with a sweet voice, but Ariel was written for Will Shakespeare's vanished Nat, the boy in his memory. You."

My aerial sprite. I shall not forget thee, Nat Field.

I couldn't speak for a moment. Whoever he was, this man, whatever he was, he leaned over me and looked in through my eyes, into the inside of my mind. "You have not lost him, Nat," he said. "You will never lose him, never."

Then he was Arby again, director, actor, teacher, boss man, dragon. He put a hand under my arm and yanked me up out of the chair. "Next summer, the Company of Boys will do a production of *The Tempest*," he said. "And you'll play Ariel. So you'd better be damn good as Puck today, or I might change my mind."

I cleared my throat, though I still sounded husky. "All right," I said.

Arby looked at me with a half-smile. I saw a muscle twitch in his cheek, below his left eye. He said, "At the end of *The Tempest* Prospero lets Ariel go free. '*I shall miss thee,*' he says, '*but still thou shalt have freedom.*' Go free, Nat—free of grieving. And your two poets will go with you always."

In the sky overhead a big jet moved across the wooden O, high up, and its distant roar rose and faded. The sound of the doves had gone.

And from the top window in the little roof house over our gallery, the long clear note of a single trumpet rang out, signaling the audience, telling the actors, calling the world to the theater. In one hour from now, our play would begin.